I0548889

The PRINCE of ACADIA & the River of Fire

J A S O N E. H A M I L T O N

Cover Design by Heather Curtis

ISBN: 9780992118983

Library and Archives Canada Cataloguing in Publication

Hamilton, Jason E., 1973-, author
   The prince of Acadia & the river of fire / Jason E. Hamilton.
Issued in print and electronic formats.
ISBN 978-0-9921189-8-3 (softcover).--ISBN 978-0-9921189-6-9 (EPUB)

      I. Title. II. Title: Prince of Acadia and the river of fire.

PS8615.A4425P75 2017   C813'.6   C2017-900544-8
                                               C2017-901559-1

To Dustin,

You were the first one to listen to the first draft. By wanting to hear the rest, you told me this was a story worth telling (sorry I didn't change the name). Thank you Sylvie for your support, even if we're two people trying to accomplish the same thing. And, of course, to you the reader, thank you for your patronage!

Contents

1

The Elderly Tyrant

"It's destroyed. Destroyed! Your son ruined my garden!"

Warren LeBlanc held the phone away from his ear. Confused. Groggy. He looked at the receiver in his hand and scratched his head. The voice continued to natter away. Warren squinted at the clock on his bedside table. 6 AM. He took a deep breath before he snuffed out the speaker and hung up.

The instant he put the phone down it rang again.

Before picking it up, Warren rolled out of bed and got to his feet. He grabbed the cordless and held it a safe distance before answering. The voice bellowed as though it was in the room. Warren winced and wished his arms were twice as long.

He shuffled down the hall. His son's door was closed. He knocked. There was no answer.

He opened the door and gazed into the room. He gasped. Somehow the person on the phone heard him.

Forceful, but not screeching, the female voice said "Now are you gonna listen to me!"

Warren gulped. He turned over the blankets on the bed. He bent down and looked underneath. He stood up, eyes studying the room. His son was nowhere to be found.

"Yes, yes," he muttered into the receiver before noticing a puff of wind ripple the curtains beside the window.

"Are you even listening?!" the shrill sound pierced the room.

"Of course," Warren said absent-mindedly as he pulled back the blinds.

"Then who am I?"

"I, uh," Warren stammered. From the window he could see directly into the shed at the rear of the house. The rolling door was up. The shed was empty.

"Now you listen to me. The damage is excessive. It's been vandalized! You're his father and I'm holding you responsible for making it right!"

Warren gulped. Now that he was fully alert he thought he recognized the voice. He wished he hadn't. He wished he could crawl back into his bed and pretend that the whole episode was just a dream. But still, he had to know for sure. Had to be absolutely certain. After all, he'd never spoken to the woman directly. But the shrill pitch was a dead giveaway. Warren stole his resolve before asking politely, "and to whom am I speaking?"

Warren regretted the answer the moment it was uttered.

"It's Hazel Inglett!"

Warren could feel his heart in his chest stop beating.

Tanner grimaced as he leaned down to pick up the wheelbarrow. His hands, drawn and worn, could not grasp the handles. The heat and sweat of the afternoon settled in his muscles. He felt centuries older than his mere twelve years. Hanging his head, his thick, blonde mane fell toward the earth. He let his body freeze in that pose, stooped over at the waist. The stretch on his hamstrings was welcome. He puffed out air from the far reaches of his soul.

"I bet that must feel good," a voice behind him observed.

Startled, Tanner jumped, lost his balance and toppled over the wheelbarrow. He shrieked, not in pain, but at the assault on his sense of smell. His cargo, a nasty assortment of rotten peelings, chicken droppings, slime and whatever else, spilled all over him.

"YUUCCKKK!!" he screamed, lying in the grime. He lay still for a moment, seething in anger. He pinched his nostrils and looked down at the mess. Egg shells. Chicken compost. Rotting fruits and vegetables. Tanner wanted to clean it all off at once but didn't know where to start.

"Oh, Tanner," the voice said, "I'm terribly sorry. I didn't mean to startle you. I just wanted to offer you a glass of lemonade."

"Gee, thanks Mrs. Inglett," he grimaced. "I hope the glass is big enough to take a bath in."

Mrs. Inglett took the handles of the wheelbarrow. With a strength that belied her age, she twisted the wreckage away from the young boy lying in the filth.

Tanner crawled out from under the heap and slowly gained his feet.

"Come along, let's get you cleaned up. You looked like you were finished for the day anyhow," she said.

"Wish I were finished for good," Tanner grumbled.

"Heh," Mrs. Inglett's ears perked. "Now listen. I didn't tell you to go vandalizing my yard with a four-wheeler. If you didn't know how to drive it, that's hardly my fault."

"But the throttle stuck open..." he pleaded.

"Not my machine, not my problem. Come along and stay

3

downwind. The last thing I want is for your father to think I've been torturing you over here." Hazel Inglett set off up the path to the elegant stately home at the top of the hill. Tanner sighed and shuffled along after her.

Tanner gritted his teeth in frustration. He had explained the story to his dad and he had explained it to Mrs. Inglett. Neither of them bought it. Even he didn't quite believe it. He knew he wasn't supposed to drive the four-wheeler by himself. He was just going to his friend's house. Riley had wanted to show him something quickly. The four-wheeler was the fastest option. It wasn't the first time Tanner had taken it without consulting his parents. But it *was* the first time the machine seemed to have a mind of its own.

No matter what he did that day, he never seemed to gain control over the machine. Steering. Speed. Brakes. He couldn't even turn it off when he wanted. And to make matters worse, his laces got wrapped around the foot pedal. By the time he had released his shoe and leapt to safety, the damage to the Inglett property had been done. The four-wheeler died out in the hedgerow. When Tanner went back to retrieve it and hopefully escape detection, the engine had refused to start. Mrs. Inglett had spontaneously appeared and he was caught red-handed.

And of all the homes, of all the people in town, it had to be a member of the Inglett family! And crazy old Hazel Inglett to boot! Ever since he was a very young boy, he knew better than to venture over to that side of town. The house was stately and elegant, but quite old. The property was immaculately kept. Despite the elaborate decorations and elegant presentation, no child dared knock on her door at Hallowe'en.

Hazel Inglett was a constant presence around town. Though

not often seen at public gatherings, she still managed to hold a great deal of influence over the small community of Whispering Cove.

Tanner was too young to know how or why her sphere of influence was as large as it was. He knew, just as sure as the tales woven by boys older than him reached his ears that the house was better left alone. And now, despite his best attempts to keep his distance, he was now in the humble service of the infamous Hazel Inglett. He sighed heavily. This was NOT how he wanted to spend his last two weeks of summer vacation.

Tanner could still hear Riley cackling with delight when he heard that Tanner had crashed the four-wheeler. Cackled because he was the one who dared him to take it in the first place. No matter how often Tanner tried to beat Riley when it came to matters of gears and gadgets, his efforts always seemed to backfire. He always seemed to get caught while Riley avoided punishment.

"I bet they're hanging out at the Sugar Shack, giggling at my expense," Tanner mumbled under his breath.

When they reached the veranda at the front of the house, Mrs. Inglett turned to address him with something resembling sympathy in her voice.

"Go around back and take off those smelly clothes. I'll get you some nice clean ones to wear. There's a garden hose attached to the garage. You can use that to get the grime and stench off you. I hope these clothes weren't your favourite. Now go on, before you stink up the rest of the place.," Mrs. Inglett marched back to her house.

Tanner followed the hose to the faucet. He leaned against the garage door and started to strip off his clothes. He was about to take off his pants when something caught his eye through the dusty garage door glass. He rubbed as much dust away as he could, not sure of what he saw.

He stole a glance over his shoulder. The coast was clear. Ever so gently, he tried the door latch. It wasn't locked. He turned the handle all the way and pushed the door. It wouldn't budge. He tried again. Again, nothing.

He took a step back to get a better grasp of things when Mrs. Inglett sent him crashing to the ground again.

"Even if you could get in, I could smell you from inside," she barked.

Tanner stammered an excuse. Normally prepared with enough confidence that would make a politician proud, he could not find the words to plead his case. Just as his thoughts were gaining traction, he was interrupted.

"That's fuhfuhfuffuhfuhfuh–FREEZZZIINGGG!!" Tanner howled as the hose water pelted his bare skin.

"Good, maybe that'll teach you to be so nosy!" Mrs. Inglett bellowed.

She tossed a bar of soap onto his chest and turned the hose away.

Tanner spat water and wiped his eyes, then stood up and started to scrub the smell of compost from his skin. He took special care not to give the garage a second glance. He'd already been busted twice by the wily old woman. It was best not to risk further humiliation. But how did she just sneak up on him like that? She seemed to appear out of thin air. He puzzled over it a moment before the feeling he was being watched stole over him. He spun around quickly. No one was there.

"I've just finished speaking to your father. He'll be here in a minute to pick you up," Mrs. Inglett declared.

Tanner spun around again. How did she do that?

"Thanks Mrs. Inglett," Tanner replied meekly.

The diesel rattle of the Volkswagen engine announced a visitor. Warren LeBlanc, Tanner's father, stepped out of the old car. He was a man of modest stature, 41 years old, balding. With his thin red beard and glasses, he could easily pass for a university professor if he dressed the part. But the calloused hands and tattered clothes showed that he earned his living doing manual labour.

Warren walked up to his son. Arms folded, he tried his best to act the part of the stern father. He scowled the right way. He furrowed his brows the right way. He huffed and puffed whenever and however he could. But Mrs. Inglett could see it was a struggle at best.

"He tries hard to pull it off," Mrs. Inglett said aloud, "but everyone can see he's an old softy!"

Warren cracked. His arms dropped to his sides as he walked up to Tanner to embrace him when he stopped in his tracks.

"You might not want to do that," Tanner advised.

He pointed at the composting clothes in the paved driveway. A hearty stench continued to waft from the stump of fabric. Warren retreated.

"On second thought… Are you ready?" Warren stepped back.

He retreated to the car, not noticing that his son hadn't joined him.

Something else caught Tanner's attention behind the shed. He peered after it. A crisp bark reminded him where he was.

"TANNER!" Warren called.

Flinching, Tanner tore himself away from his curiosity and ran to the awaiting car.

7

Mrs. Inglett shuffled up the steps to her porch before she looked at her smartphone. She swiped at the screen, a new image flipping under her fingers. A sepia portrait, mined from an old photo album and digitally scanned, rested in her hands.

"Hard to believe a photo over a hundred years old could still be so clear," she wondered aloud to herself. A few more pictures flashed in front of her before she stopped on the overturned wheelbarrow. She chuckled to herself. She passed over several before noticing Tanner get in the car.

"William would have been his age." She stifled a sob.

From her vantage point, she could see Warren dominating the conversation in the car. Tanner's head hung low. Warren stopped talking for a minute while he waited for a response from his son. Tanner's mouth barely moved. Warren sighed before creeping backwards out of the driveway.

"And just as mischievous. I'll need to be careful with him."

As the car backed away, Mrs. Inglett stuffed the smartphone carefully into its holder on her hip.

The car was barely on the road when Warren continued his mild interrogation.

"Did you do everything Mrs. Inglett asked you to do?"

"Yes, Dad," Tanner replied sheepishly.

"Did you give her any backtalk?"

"No."

"Any grief of any kind?"

"Nope."

"Really?"

"Yeah, Dad, sheesh."

"Really, because that's not how she tells it."

"Uh, what?" Tanner stammered.

Warren waited a minute. He'd heard nothing of the kind, but in his dealings with his son, he knew how to get a confession out of him.

"Okay Dad, I saw something in her garage. Something really odd. Dad, she's weird," Tanner started.

"I know she is Tanner. But that's not the point. The point is that it's someone else's things and property and you should respect it."

"Sorry, Dad."

"Apology accepted. Now please don't do it again."

The rest of the ride home the car remained silent. Warren wanted desperately to understand his son. The child seemed to have no concept of boundaries. No idea where and when he should harness his inquisition. Tanner was always a naturally curious child. Constantly getting tangled in this mess and that. Much as he wanted, nothing Warren could do was ever going to change that.

He wasn't a malicious kid. His intentions, so far as Warren could understand, always came from a place of general inquisitiveness. Warren was inspired to see such curiosity in his child when he was younger. Was that curiosity starting to become problematic? The four-wheeler mishap certainly suggested that. But the end result wasn't something Tanner was typically known for. If anything, Warren was prepared to get a phone call from a local farmer to rescue his son who had run out of gas at an abandoned quarry.

The day Warren got the call from Hazel Inglett, he somehow knew his son crossed a line. When he arrived at the property to survey the damage, he was taken aback at how extensive it was. The impressive hedgerow that lined the driveway was almost completely uprooted. The beautiful flower garden, an attraction for visitors from out of town, was a disheveled mess. It looked more like the aftermath of a demolition derby than the famed English gardens that inspired it.

Mrs. Inglett, in her wisdom, let the damage speak for itself. She knew only too well the grip her reputation had on the rest of the townsfolk. It wasn't long before the entire town was buzzing with news of Tanner's transgression. Not so much WHAT had happened, but who was the poor soul to risk her wrath. And yet, how much of her reputation was deserved and how much was fabrication? Only Hazel Inglett, a spirited, widowed 67 year old who behaved like she was 27, knew the answer to both.

She could have asked for significant monetary compensation. No one would have even been surprised if she took a page out of Shakespeare and asked for a pound of flesh. Warren didn't exactly go into the negotiation holding a strong hand. But much to his surprise, the woman seemed quite understanding. It seemed so out of line with her reputation. Warren was only too grateful not to have him or his son working for the rest of their lives to repair the damage. In fact, a twelve year-old boy working for just two weeks didn't seem nearly enough to begin to fix the problem. Was there another reason for her leniency? Warren was still mulling it over as he pulled the old Volkswagen to a stop.

Tanner scampered out of the car and into the house. He breezed past his mother and went straight to his room. Warren followed him into the house to see his wife looking frazzled.

"Hmm, the Flash must have come this way..."

"Tornado more like it."

Warren was about to bellow out again when his wife held her

hand to his lips.

"Did you talk to him about your idea?"

"It was a short drive. There wasn't enough time."

"Have you talked to the other Dads?

"I have. They all love it. Except Marshal, of course. His phone told me he might not be here. Probably in Dubai that week-end."

"Or Singapore."

"Tokyo maybe…"

2

The Strange Tourist

"He gave them the four-wheeler. Marshal gave Donovan the keys for his eleventh birthday. Eleven!!"

"I know. It was a little young."

"A little! If Tanner and Riley weren't so, so, so…"

"Rambunctious."

"Yup. Then it wouldn't be so bad. In fact, I bet Donovan would hardly ever take it out of the baby barn."

"Probably."

The men stared off in silence. Leaning against the garage door jamb, Roy sipped from his cup.

"Then if we're gonna do this, we're gonna do this."

"Can you really get all the equipment?"

"Absolutely. Cripes, I've got half of it in my garage. I thought I'd hold onto it. There aren't a lot of guys who do Special Effects around here. My wife convinced me to keep as much as I could. Y'know, in case a big film does blow into Acadia and sets up shop," Roy explained.

He stared off for a moment. Warren could read his thoughts.

"You miss show business, don't you?" Warren finally said.

"Huh? Oh. Well, it isn't so much that, really. But, we did

move here because I thought it would be a better place for Riley to grow up. And now that he keeps getting into trouble.... I expected that in L. A. Not in Acadia."

"That's why this is so important now, don't you see? We're as much shaped by our community and peers as we are by our family. And what is our community doing? They're on the computer. Or playing video games. Boys aren't meant for that. Boys need dirt under their fingernails. Boys need bruises and cuts. Chafes and twigs stuck in their hair. Tanner needs the steadying influence of a hands-on Dad who not only remembers what it was like to be young, but can help him navigate those difficult waters. Riley and Donovan do, too. This will help give them that boost of confidence."

"Okay. Right. I get it. You handle the philosophy of all this and I'll deal with the nuts and bolts. What do you want? I can make wind, fire, smoke, rain, snow. Whatever. Give me a few days to get some things set up. We can do it all."

"Really? All of that?"

"Oh yeah. I was a top L. A. F/X man for ten years. I've built it up and torn it apart more times than you can count."

"Well. That changes things. I wasn't thinking quite that elaborate..."

"Hey, if we're gonna do this, what better way than to show our kids how to go all out? You wanna 'test' 'em? Let's test 'em!"

Warren studied Roy for a moment. They were both about the same age, but that was where the similarities ended. Roy was a complete gear-head. A heavy metal nut even into his early forties. The first time they had met, Roy boasted to Warren that he was making a special trip to Boston to catch a Metallica concert. Roy even went so far as to muse aloud about having his stepson, then only nine years old, accompany him. The style of the music didn't seem to faze his thinking. Warren only managed to get Roy to reconsider with the idea he might be exposing Riley to the sight of illegal activities. Roy meant no harm, of course, but Warren wondered what other parental judgment calls his friend had let slide.

His Hollywood background and devil-may-care attitude naturally brought Roy a lot of attention during his short time in Whispering Cove. Initially, he had enjoyed it. He even played it up a little. Blowing up birthday cakes and sabotaging pools with dish soap. It was all in good fun and no harm had been done. (Okay, maybe an eyebrow or two was singed at Chester Brown's birthday party.) But Whispering Cove did not take kindly to such antics. It was only through the charm of his wife, Chantale, that Roy and Riley made any friends at all.

"Okay, just don't go crazy, alright?"

"Who, me?" Roy acted hurt.

"Uh, remember Chester Brown's birthday party?"

"How could I forget? That stuffed shirt never saw it coming," Roy boasted.

"He wasn't the only one who never saw it coming," Warren agreed and chuckled.

"Let's also keep in mind that our kids are only twelve. It's meant to be designed in a way to test them. To get them to think for themselves and trust their instincts."

"Alrighty then, you want gear. You want Special Effects equipment. You want obstacles and challenges, does that sound right?" Roy confirmed.

"Yes, absolutely," Warren nodded.

"Where? How? Have you thought about that?" Roy asked.

"I have a friend of mine with a good chunk of property upriver.

I've known him a long time. Once I tell him my idea, I'm sure he won't mind if we use it," Warren said.

"Will this be aquatic? Will there be a map? What kind of tools will the boys be allowed to have? What safety measures have you put in place?"

"Er, I guess I didn't think of any of that," Warren confessed.

"Contrary to popular belief, I am not hiding out in Whispering Cove because I orchestrated an effect that went horribly wrong and injured someone. I was— I AM—incredibly good at my craft. I am completely safety conscious. Especially when it comes to the welfare of my stepson," Roy said.

Warren shook his head in disbelief.

"I know. It seems hard to believe doesn't it? I was the guy who took him to the shooting range for his ninth birthday," Roy agreed.

"You better believe it. And sorry, I haven't given the specifics of the challenge that much thought," Warren said.

"When all else fails, consult the internet," Roy said.

He opened the door to his garage. He flicked on the light and motioned Warren to join him at the bench where his laptop lay. The garage was immaculately organized. The entire outer walled was rimmed with shelving. On the shelving were clear plastic bins. The facing of the shelves were labeled, as were the plastic containers. The floor was clean and dry.

"Wow, this is cleaner than my house," Warren confessed.

"Don't get used to it. Most of my stuff is in a trailer. And the trailer is a disaster. My wife likes to use the garage as a gym. She won't stand anything that's disorganized and messy," Roy said.

Warren, as curious as his son, explored the shelving like it was his own house.

"Do you value your life? If the missus catches you..."

Warren backed away and stammered, "I- I- I was just wondering..."

"I'm messing with you. My house is your house. You're wondering if I have any camping gear, aren't you?"

"I've got some gear to go camping and fishing, but not enough for all three boys."

"You fish? You never mentioned that before."

"C'mon Roy, EVERYBODY here fishes."

"I just never heard you mention it that's all. And I've never heard you brag either."

"Well, that's not my style."

The truth was Warren didn't really fish. He liked to use the guise of fishing to traverse deep into the woods. Once there, he practiced deep meditation. It was a ritual he started the year he moved back to Acadia. He brought a few friends with him when he returned in his early twenties, friends who wanted desperately to live simpler lives. Lives free from much of the material trappings of the previous generation.

Warren convinced ten of his college friends that land in Acadia was cheap to acquire and the perfect place to put some of their ideas into practice: build their own home and grow their own food. Get back to the land. Two of them didn't finish the first month. After six months, only four of them remained.

Warren was accustomed to the physical demands of carving out a life from the land. His friends were initially enthusiastic as well. The joy and elation of building a homestead gave way to the more challenging reality of learning to share responsibilities and chores. It surprised him to learn that his friends, most of them raised in the comfort of suburbia, excelled at the physical work required to tend fields. Where the enterprise fell apart was in personal management. Bickering gave way to deep-rooted resentment. The resentment became a chasm that couldn't be overcome. Or maybe it was the isolation, mosquitoes and black flies?

Warren found his peace and didn't look back. He stayed and made a life for himself. But somehow the joy of fishing still managed to elude him.

"Don't feel bad," I haven't taken to fishing yet either," Roy confessed, "I don't have any outdoor gear at all."

"Nothing?" Warren asked.

"Maybe a sleeping bag. And it's so tattered and worn the boys won't want to touch it, much less use it," Roy added.

"I doubt Marshal will have anything," Warren said.

Roy guffawed. Warren joined him.

"Yup, that's what I thought too."

"He barely has an emergency safety kit in his BMW. I highly doubt those hands have touched a night crawler in thirty years," Roy chided.

"Looks like we need to do some shopping."

The car eased into the parking lot of the department store. The day was brisk. The lot was full. Hugging the sea, close to warm beaches and content travelers, Whispering Cove was a bustle of activity even into late summer. Main Street was a modest affair. Small businesses, catering to the transient population, dotted the boulevard: frozen yogurt stands, swimwear shops, art shacks. A few wooden patios, temporary structures that could be dismantled when the season wrapped up, jutted out into the parking lane.

Cars moved slowly. Pedestrians at a brisk pace could easily

keep up. The tourists didn't seem to mind, happy and content to while away the time. To the locals, who needed to navigate the slowly moving traffic to get to the other end of town, patience was often in short supply. The town was designed to support a small population. That population exploded in size during the bustling summer months.

Roy and Warren slipped out of the car and walked toward the department store.

"A solar oven? What if it rains?" Roy asked as the door opened and both men marched inside.

"Maybe we should let the boys figure out what they need?" Warren asserted.

"If we leave it up to them, they'd buy two days' worth of chips, soda and chocolate bars," Roy said.

As the two of them stood in the aisle, a short, silver-haired man brushed past them. He walked with a purpose in his stride. He had a force about him that was impossible to ignore. Had Warren been one step further into the aisle, he'd have been bowled over. Startled, he stepped back and eyed the man who thundered past him.

"Tourists," Roy muttered as the man, still driven, reached the end of the aisle and turned abruptly to his right.

Both men could hear the man talking to himself as he charged around the store.

"He doesn't look like any tourist I've ever seen," Warren observed.

His heavy steps echoed throughout the store. As other customers walked past, they shuddered at each footfall. Roy noticed small globs of reddish-grey mud that seemed to crumble and jump with each impact. The man made no effort to conceal his grime and gruff. He took over the entire aisle as his

18

eyes pored over items on the shelf. As other patrons shuffled past, they made sure to give the man a wide berth.

"Long sleeves in the middle of summer. Work boots. I don't think his intentions are leisurely," Roy agreed.

Puzzled, yet unconcerned, both men returned their attention to shopping.

3

Inside the Sugar Shack

In another pocket of Acadian wilderness, set deep into a dense patch of mixed forest, a weathered shack struggled against the test of time. Heavy snow loads, wind and other elements left it shrugged into the clay soil. The roof, rusted steel in some places, moss-covered in others, managed to hold its dignity and purpose under the branches and leaves that threatened to engulf it. But make no mistake, despite its unkempt outer appearance, the structure was built with a rugged definition that allowed it to stand for over a hundred years. Or so it was thought. When Warren bought the small patch of land from the old farmer who owned the property, even he couldn't recall it ever not being there.

It had long ago finished its role as a functioning sugar shack. In later years, the area around the shack had become a gathering ground for old, worn-out farm equipment. Tractors, wagons, harvesters, and other tools were pulled to the forest and forgotten. For a young boy with an active imagination, such mysterious gear was a natural place for his adventurous spirit to grow. Tanner loved the small, hidden spaces. Games were easy to conjure and act out. It was during one of those play sessions that he managed to sneak into the old sugar shack.

When he saw the chance to turn the place into a fort for him and his friends, Warren warmed to the idea when he saw how cozy and sturdy the old structure remained. In short order, with help from his buddies, they'd managed to convert the old sugar shack into something of a headquarters. It was just far enough away that the boys had the space and time to be boys, but close enough that if a disagreement turned heated a parent could quell the dust-up.

But what the parents weren't aware of was the boys had made a few alterations both inside and out of the old sugar shack. Tanner's friend Donovan, who was fond of research and science, had been listening to a radio show about an old woodsman who had disintegrated a tree with a crash of his hand. What he'd come to learn was that under certain conditions, a birch tree would go completely hollow from insects and disease. From the vast forest near Tanner's house, the boys sought a few of those hollowed out logs and managed to muscle them up to the sugar shack with the help of Donovan's four wheeler. Lying in and amongst a pile of other logs abutting the shack, no one knew it was a tunnel up to the edge of the wall. Under the floor of the shack, a small hatch was carved and the boys created their very own secret entrance. The old farm equipment that littered the yard around the shack also managed to conceal it away from prying eyes.

Inside was a different story. What started out as an install of a wireless Internet connection and modest electrical power had turned into a more involved project. A few solar panels were added to the roof to collect sun-rays and feed a battery bank to power the electronic gadgets the boys used. Somewhere along the way, a satellite dish was added to a clearing and the modest sugar shack turned into a hi-tech bunker in the woods. The initial battery bank was expanded and the boys were equipped with lighting and surveillance equipment for their modest enterprise.

"They want us to do what?" Riley exclaimed. Taller than the rest of the boys, Riley Matisse was the hands-on orchestrator of much that had been accomplished in the short amount of time the boys had taken up residence in the sugar shack. Constantly in the hip pocket of his stepfather, Riley had become accustomed to manipulating the various gadgets and tools in Roy's repertoire.

"A ritual," Donovan said, barely lifting his eyes from the screen. While Riley had the mechanical know-how to put their lavish ideas into practice, Donovan was the chief architect when it came to planning it all out. He'd managed to locate the optimum spot for the positioning of the satellite dish and a rough design to provide enough power and lighting for their headquarters.

Ever since news slipped the dads had come up with the scheme, they'd been very tight-lipped with their sons. The challenge had a purpose. The purpose was to get the boys to think for themselves as they encountered various obstacles along the river. Any further information would give them too much of an advantage. They were not allowed to scout, cheat, sneak or in any other way know what the 'challenge' would be all about.

"A rite of passage," Tanner corrected them as he squeezed through the trapdoor, "according to my Dad, there are too many distractions for us to really know when we've begun the journey into adulthood.....or something like that."

"And the ancient cultures recognized this significant development in a person's life and devised a 'rite of passage' to test and push them to see if they were ready for the real challenge of adulthood," Donovan explained

Tanner and Riley turned to look at Donovan. Looking up from his phone, he finally noticed their stares. He smiled shyly before turning the phone for them to see the words on the screen. "At least, that's what it says here."

"Is your dad okay with that?" Riley asked.

"Far as I know..." Donovan mumbled before his ears perked up, "Wait, I've got a great idea, let's ask him."

Donovan sat perched in what he liked to call the 'Crow's Nest'. It was the information hub of the entire sugar shack. Three screens could be dialed in on radial arms or moved away. One flat screen contained the camera feeds from various points in the forest. The other two were a real time feed of their current activities, everything from gaming to homework. The rest of the information hub was a collection of drives and inputs from tape to DVD to everything in between.

Donovan's father, Marshal, was a bit of a mystery to the other two boys. Even Tanner, the most inquisitive of the three, hadn't been able to fully understand what Marshal did with his time. Donovan, shy and intelligent, didn't ask that many questions. The only thing he knew was his father seemed to trek around the globe on business. When he wasn't travelling, Marshal Caine wasn't very far removed from his smartphone. The best intelligence Marshal could give them was that he was in the import/export business.

In the time it took the two boys to cross the floor, Donovan flipped through a few screens to video calling. In no time Marshal Caine appeared on the screen.

"I wonder where he is this time?" Riley whispered to Tanner.

Donovan started to shake his screen, "What's going on? There seems to be fog."

"Stop shaking the phone, son. I'm in a Japanese sauna. I haven't got much time until my contact arrives. If this is about Tanner's Dad's, uh, idea, then yes, I'm all for it. It will be good for you boys. Although I don't know why they won't let you have a GPS."

"No GPS?"

"No technology."

"Nothing!?!"

"No. Look, son, I don't know if it's a good idea, either. Just sit tight. I should be able to get home in time before you go on this wild adventure. Okay, I love you. Gotta go!" Marshal said and the screen went blank.

"Wow. Didja hear that guys? No technology," Donovan said and slumped in his chair.

"Ugghh. Alone in the woods. Won't that be a challenge enough?"

The boys murmured a little. Much as the Sugar Shack seemed like a good idea, not all of the dads could come to a consensus on the limit of technology. Warren was the most steadfast on keeping the place rustic and simple. Marshal was able to convince Warren that they could also use the technology to keep an eye on their kids. He explained how he was able to impose limitations on their surfing habits and contact with risky and restricted sights.

"Come on. It's camping in the woods. I've been doing it since I've been in diapers," Tanner said, "and now it will just be us. We can do this, we can show them what we're really made of!"

"Blood and guts?" offered Riley.

"We're a multi-celled organism of independent brain capacity and consciousness?" Donovan said.

"Come on. We just have to pass the time in the woods in a tent for a couple of nights. We'll bring a guitar. Sing some songs. Tell some stories. I'm sure that's all they have planned. It's not like we'll have to fish for our own food and forage for our own berries. They wouldn't go that extreme, would they?"

"All my dad ever does when he goes camping is drink beer and fart a lot," Riley said.

"I'll bring the beans!" Donovan chimed.

"Guys, come on. Let's do this. Let's show our dads what we're made of. We don't need the internet and video games to entertain ourselves. We're smart and we have great imaginations," Tanner continued.

"Okay then, Mr. Smarty-pants, what campfire songs do you know?" Riley countered.

"Uh... uh..." Tanner stuttered.

"Just what I thought."

"Well hey, no one says we can't use the internet to our advantage BEFORE we go camping," Tanner said and scurried over to the Crow's Nest.

"Is Roy Jones, the famous Special Effects Coordinator going to call in a favour and have us helicoptered into the challenge area?" Donovan asked.

"My dad?" Riley asked. "Are you sure about that?"

"Check it out."

The light flickered on the screen. A grainy video depicted a close-up of what appeared to be Roy Jones. He stood at attention as action buzzed around him. A raid of some kind. Helicopters swirled in the distance. The wind whipped up dust and debris as Roy held the walkie-talkie close to his lips. The howling intensity didn't seem to faze him. He didn't flinch as around him, through the massive lightning flashes, rain pelted the helicopter.

Roy waved his hands: a series of explosions detonated all around the helicopter. Massive fireballs licked into the air. Sparks and puffs of smoke echoed around the screen.

"CUT! CUT! CUT!"

The howling wind died down. The rain, which had almost streamed sideways, drizzled from a metal tower. The helicopter touched down in the middle of the set. The swirling blades slowed.

"Nice work, boys!" Roy bellowed into the walkie-talkie.

As the blades of the helicopter slowed to a stop, more people spilled from all corners of the camera. From the ground, prone bodies dressed in full military camouflage rose from the dead.

"We nailed it!"

The boys stared at the screen, eyes wide, mouths agape.

"Any of you guys recognize that movie?" Donovan asked.

"Nope." Tanner responded. "Jeez, Riley, you never told me your dad did cool stuff like that. Think he'll have a camera set up for when we go through the obstacles?"

"I never thought to ask him," Riley confessed.

"That would be awesome!"

"Okay, alright, but that still doesn't tell us anything. I highly doubt we're going to be airlifted into the middle of a combat zone, even a fake one," Donovan mused.

"And don't forget, my dad's involved in this, too," Tanner said.

"Yeah, there'll probably be some basket-making challenge," Riley teased.

"Or we'll have to make a bird house from drift wood," Donovan giggled.

"Alright, okay, I get it. Very funny," Tanner muttered before looking directly at Donovan. "At least my dad's around when I need him."

The room fell into silence. Donovan glowered at Tanner before taking a swipe at his friend.

Tanner stepped back from the monitors. He crouched, ready for a confrontation. Donovan hopped off the chair casually. He leaned back against the desk and flipped the hair from his eyes. Riley was quick to intervene. He waded between his two friends and kept them both at arms' distance.

"Oops, somebody crossed the line. Tanner, I think you better apologize," Riley said.

Tanner took a deep breath and hung his head. "I'm sorry, DC," he said to the floor. Donovan gritted his teeth.

"Okay guys, shake hands," Riley commanded. Tanner extended his hand. Donovan took it.

"Great. Are we all good now? Awesome, let's get on with it."

Riley eased into the swiveling captain's chair and took command. Donovan quickly found his sense of humour. "I never expected YOU would be the peacemaker."

"And I never expected I'd get a chance in the Captain's Chair," Riley responded, "How do you work this thing again?"

Donovan sighed and stood beside his friend. The three boys gathered around the Crow's Nest. The rite of passage had begun.

4

Footsteps at the Rivers' Edge

Warrens' hands gripped the steering wheel of his old car. The back swerved and bounced with each washboard section of gravel road. As the rattling intensified, he finally relented. The car couldn't take the abuse anymore. He pulled the Volkswagen to a stop and heaved a sigh of relief. The clattering of his teeth finally subsided. He thought he knew the way well enough, but with the overgrowth and canopy, he wasn't entirely sure how far ahead the camp rested. It was only when he got out of the car and looked up and down the road that he realized how long it had been since he last travelled the secluded road.

Roy promised he had everything they would need. Hopefully all his equipment made it down in one piece. Warren got out and stood on a small crest on the gravel road. Ahead in the distance, a small plume of smoke wafted above the tree line.

His old car wasn't meant to handle such rough terrain. He needed to investigate the rest of the road to determine if he should keep driving and risk damaging his car, or walk the rest of the way. The first thing he noticed was a deep rut that crossed the tire path at the top of the hill. The heavy rain that had plunged through the area a few days ago had left a deep scar on the road. The top of the hill was dry now, but a little remaining water trickled into the culvert. Rushing water crossed under the gravel road at the bottom of the incline. If he were to keep driving, he'd have to go low and slow.

He considered walking. In the last great heat of the summer, the mosquitoes could sense prey. He couldn't remember how much farther he needed to go to reach the camp. If he did walk, he'd have company. Lingering was not an option either. The rain left the encroaching foliage lousy with hungry critters. His only hope was for the road conditions to relent and smooth out at the next hill.

As he stood alone beside his car, the swaying branches and buzzing mosquitoes prevented him from hearing the heavy commotion behind him. A massive rig, rattling, clanging and speeding along the same path, startled Warren when it belched over the same hill he was standing on. Surprised, he jumped into a heap of blackberry bushes, promptly lost his footing and tumbled into a ditch. Over rocks, long grass and a groundhog hole, Warren rolled and flailed. His limbs clacked and banged on the way down.

He stopped in a mess of ferns and wild mushrooms.

Warren took a deep breath, blowing dust and grass high into the air. Nicked, scraped and mildly punctured, Warren took a mental account of his situation.

"Whew," he said to the incessantly buzzing mosquitoes that he managed to stir up with his fall. "I guess if I just lay here and think about it, I'll get eaten alive." He shook his extremities. "Everything seems to be working fine."

Grabbing at the first sturdy branch above him, he pulled and tugged until he could crawl out of the ditch. A dispersing cloud of dust that the truck had stirred was all that was left of his encounter. He could hear the faint rumblings of its engine in the distance.

"What would a tanker truck be doing on a backwoods road like this?"

Warren marched on. His feet stumbled up and over deep ruts. The late afternoon heat clung to the small of his back. He walked slowly, training his ears for any repeat approach of a transport truck. He trudged up another hill and bend in the road before he finally reached the camp.

It was all peace and solitude as Warren approached Harry's camp. He turned the corner of the modest home and expected to find his friend splayed out on his Muskoka chair, fast asleep, book in hand and fishing rod at his side.

But when Warren started clomping around to announce his presence, the empty chair rested at the water's edge. No book. No fishing rod. No sign of Harry at all.

Warren shuffled his feet and opened the screen door with a rusty creak.

The main door was locked. He peered through the open window. No lights were on. The place looked completely undisturbed.

As a village elder in the local Mi'kmaq tribe, Harry was quite often busy. He was well known in Whispering Cove and maintained an open door policy to all. He openly boasted that he had nothing to hide or steal and deliberately kept his door unlocked. The last thing he wanted, he explained one day to Warren, was to turn away a troubled kid because his door was barred shut.

Since Warren, Marshal and Roy had informed Harry of their

plans, Warren had assumed that the elder would be along shortly. Until then, Warren needed to scout the land he once knew so well to plan the obstacles and challenges.

Warren marched down the gently sloping ground in the comfortable shade of a massive willow tree toward the edge of the water and made the yodeling sound only Harry would recognize from their childhood.

"Yoawkahoo!"

His voice echoed off the water and bluff on the other side of the river. There was no response from Harry.

Warren knew the camp well enough. Knew the layout of the river up and downstream. Like a cagey movie director, he set to envisioning the obstacles and challenges he wanted to create for Tanner and his friends. He marched up and down the edge of the river, completely lost in his thoughts. Had he taken a moment, he might have noticed the muddy tracks that sprang up from the front of the Muskoka chair. Those same tracks indented the soil as they approached the river's edge.

Warren walked right up to the edge of the water and stood in the exact same spot his friend had only a few hours before. Had he not been so distracted, he would have seen that Harry's footprints continued in the water through the shallow muddy clay toward the middle of the river.

But Warren saw no sign of Harry's movements. He was preoccupied, trying his best to determine where the smoke machines were going to go. Could a rain tower be rigged to disappear? Where would they hide the giant fans responsible for the heavy winds? Were they going for the element of surprise? How would they operate all the equipment? Warren and Roy were a team of two. Could they handle everything by themselves?

He was starting to have second thoughts. It was all well and good to talk about doing something elaborate. Executing the idea was another matter entirely. Fortunately, the mystery of what could be achieved seemed to energize the boys. They were looking forward to it. The more insistent the boys became to figure out what their dads were up to, the more pressure there was to create something worthwhile.

"How long will it be before they figure it out?"

"Oh, if I know the boys like I think I do they've probably got our exact location pinpointed on Google Earth. They'll have researched all of the equipment and know a lot more about what we're doing than we do," Roy confessed.

"Wow, you really think so?" Warren asked.

"Why not? You can find practically everything you want on the Internet. Well, those of us that know WHAT they're looking for, anyway," Roy chuckled.

"Geez, should we even bother then?"

"It's like standing in the batters box against Nolan Ryan. You might know WHAT he's going to throw. Hell, everyone in the stadium knew that. But you still have to get in there and actually hit it. The boys may know exactly what gear we're using, but they still have to figure out how it works and find a solution to the obstacles," Roy countered.

Warren considered that for a moment.

"Think of it as the difference between theory and practice."

Warren, buoyed by the confidence of his partner, felt his posture straighten slightly.

"That makes sense. Alrighty then, let's do this!" he exclaimed and slapped Roy on the back.

Roy looked at him quizzically before walking to the back of the trailer.

"Hmm, the contents might have shifted during flight. That was one bumpy road."

Warren stooped to look at the wheels. The bottom of the trailer hung painfully low.

"Yikes. I think the contents might be under pressure. Let's be safe about this."

"Warren, stand back."

Roy angled his body away from the doors. He spun the key. A deep creaking noise came from inside before both doors flung open with a heavy bang. The two men dove into the grass and covered their heads as a single clamp sprang into the air before falling to the ground. They sat up as the load stayed rooted in place, pushing against a safety rail at the back of the trailer.

"That wasn't so bad," Roy offered.

"Let's hope the rest of it isn't vacuum sealed."

"If we pull something out of there, the whole thing is going to burst out at us. Don't you have a side door or something?" Warren asked.

Roy shook his head.

"How about a helmet?"

A loud crack split the air. Warren ducked. "She's gonna blow!"

Warren cowered and covered his head. Roy didn't budge.

When Warren stood, he saw his friend holding a smoking cap gun.

"Works every time. You should've seen the look on your face!" Roy doubled over, laughing.

Warren shook his head. Maybe if he loosened up a little, Roy might not trick him so easily.

"Those carts are going to move first. Stick your foot under the tire to keep it from rolling," Roy instructed.

"Haven't you got something else to wedge in there? I'd rather it wasn't my foot."

"You'll be fine. Simple physics."

Roy released the safety bar.

"That's heavy! What is this stuff, anyway?" Warren asked.

Roy pushed the cart forward and off of Warren's foot.

"This cart has about a thousand feet of inch and a half water hose. I hope your friend has good water pressure here."

"I think so. He was supposed to meet us, but I haven't seen him," Warren confided.

"You said yourself that people come to him all the time for help," Roy said.

"And some need more help than others..."

"There you go. Quit worrying! Seriously, man, I've been in Whispering Cove almost three years and in that time the most I've ever had to worry about is teenagers joyriding on a Sunday afternoon," Roy said.

"What about Saturday night?"

"Dude, I'm in bed on Saturday nights," Roy said and hoisted a ramp onto the back of the trailer, "I don't know what you're up to."

Warren sighed and edged the heavy metal cart to the back of the trailer.

"If you don't know what you're doing, jump out of the way," Roy said.

Warren turned, slightly confused. The weight of the cart was starting to lean on him. He pushed forward, trying to make space. If he tried to jump out of the way, he might not make it to safety in time. Roy was offering no help. He stood on the ground, out of the trailer, arms folded across his chest.

Warren noticed Roy's tendons move in his forearm. It was as though he had something in his hand and was going to play another joke.

The cart inched out of the trailer. Warren looked at Roy. The hint of a grin tugged at the corner of his mouth. The incline increased and it was all Warren could do to keep the cart and its contents from hurtling down the ramp and him under it. Sweat dripped from his brow.

"Like I said, Warren, if you don't know what you're doing, jump out of the way," Roy said, his voice slow and deliberate.

"Why did you let me?"

"You were there first and you seemed to know what you were doing..."

Warren looked away. If he could concentrate on something else, maybe the cart wouldn't feel so heavy. He was absolutely certain Roy was playing another trick on him. Was he going to pop a plastic bag? Shoot the cap gun again?

Unable to take the strain any longer, Warren scoured the grass for an ideal place to land. Confident he found one, he turned as if to leap. Roy shielded his eyes. Warren stopped dead in his tracks and quietly raised his hands from the cart. It didn't budge an inch.

The large rubber wheels had lodged themselves against the edges of the ramp.

"Gotcha!" Warren sauntered down the corrugated steel ramp.

"Sneaky," Roy said. Both men heard a loud bang and a groan. They looked at one another. Each man pleaded their innocence. One wheel sprung free and the entire cart hurtled down the gate.

It continued down the gentle slope toward the water's edge.

The only thing that kept the whole mess from spilling into the river was the sloppy clay and earth at the edge of the waterway. Both men giggled as they pulled themselves to their feet.

They walked to the edge of the water to retrieve the cart.

Had they stopped giggling, they might have noticed something odd near the edge of the tires. In the rut caused by the weight of the cart, small pools of water rushed in to fill the space. The water seemed to be eating away at the tires. The dry rubber started to look slick and shiny. The pool of water was beginning to slowly darken. A layer of black rubber had been eaten away. A thin film was mixing with the water.

Roy and Warren rescued the cart before either of them noticed anything of consequence.

5

Trouble at Rocky Point Wharf

"Hey, check it out, my dad figured out how to Instant Message," Riley chortled.

"Did he say more than just 'hi'?"

"Uh, Donovan, can you help me out with this?"

Riley handed his cell phone to Donovan. Donovan palmed the device for a moment. He plugged it into his laptop and before long the extent of the message was splashed across the large screen in the centre of the array.

"Boys. The River of Fire is the spiritual home of the Mi'kmaq. It was a critical facet of their lives. In the summer, the tribe would follow the tides to the mouth of the river. There they would live on the abundant shellfish and rich marine life at the edge of the coast. When the changing winds started to blow, the Mi'kmaq could feel the imminent change of the season.

"At the end of the summer, riding the tides, traders would travel far upstream to the very birth of the river. They would cross to a branch of the south-flowing waters until they came upon their neighbours. They would trade goods, exchange stories and reap the benefits of a good season.

"The goal of your journey is to follow that spiritual path to its source. In part, this is the essence of your own journey. As the various challenges greet you along the way, you will discover reserves and resources within that you never knew you had. We will push you to confront both your fears and flaws. When you are finished with the rite of passage you won't be the same.

"**Donovan**: you are extremely intelligent behind a screen. You can manipulate a computer with tremendous skill. You will discover you have talents beyond that when you allow yourself the confidence to step out from behind the monitor."

"**Riley**: you have so much confidence it borders on arrogance. This doesn't allow your friends to participate and add their perspective. It can push them away. Look for an opportunity to show humility. The learning experience will be tremendous."

"**Tanner:** we are only too aware of what brought about this adventure in the first place. Your curiosity as a child seemed to know no bounds. Unfortunately, there is a bad side to that trait. You have a habit of acting first without thinking about consequences. Focus that inquisitiveness and it will serve you well."

"See, I told you this wasn't just going to be singing songs in the woods," Riley muttered as they finished reading the message.

"Like the ancient Mi'kmaq traders, your journey will begin at the mouth of the River of Fire."

It was the middle of a hot late summer afternoon when Tanner, Riley and Donovan arrived at the dunes. Tanner's grandfather, a spry man in his early seventies, drove the truck as far out onto the beach as the road would allow.

As the beaten grasses gave way to gently rising sand hills,

Oland LeBlanc pulled the truck to a stop. Reluctantly, the doors opened and the boys spilled out of the vehicle.

Whoops and cries from the nearby beach only illustrated the fun that the boys were missing out on. They slowly opened the tailgate.

"You HAD to crash the four-wheeler!" Riley lamented. Tanner ignored his friend as he harnessed his backpack over his shoulders and marched over the dune. Donovan and Riley said nothing as they followed their friend.

Oland smirked to himself at the sight of his grandson about to embark on his great adventure. Rather than speed off, he reached into the front seat for his fishing rod. He leaned it against the side of the truck before retrieving his CB radio.

"Huck Finn to Tom Sawyer, repeat, Huck Finn to Tom Sawyer. The Three Investigators have left the shuttle. Repeat, the Three Investigators have left the shuttle."

"Copy that, Huck Finn!"

Oland took his rod and a small fishing tackle and followed the path blazed by his grandson. Always watchful and concerned, the elder LeBlanc wanted to make sure the boys started the adventure unscathed.

The sun was high in the sky, slowly starting to retreat along the horizon. From the river, the occasional burr and hum of a powerboat shook their senses. At the crest of the dune, the boys watched a stream of leisurely adventurers parade past along the edge of the ocean: Sea-Doo's, water skiers and others their own age rejoiced in the speed of the open river as it brushed the ocean. Longing for the carefree revelry, the boys couldn't help but sigh.

"Oh man, how unfair is this? We're gonna be stuck on the stupid river in a birch bark canoe!" Riley fired.

"Now, come on guys, they wouldn't go that far...would they?" Donovan said.

The other two turned to look at him.

"Think about it. They're dads. They're busy doing Dad stuff and don't have time for something like that," Donovan defended, "And they've got the obstacle course they're making."

A little reassured, the boys trudged on. A few moments passed before they realized they were moving farther away from the throngs of people along the coast. The gentle slopes of sand started to dwindle. Beach grass, like rough stubble, poked through the sand and lashed at their legs.

The boys marched farther into the wilderness with Tanner holding a rudimentary map. So far, the adventure was like Geo-caching. The style was deliberate.

"Do you think this is part of the....?"

"Ritual. Game. Challenge."

"Well, they did talk about how the Mi'kmaq used to live off of shellfish."

"Do you have anything to dig and collect clams?"

"Did we even bother to look at the packs to see what we have to work with?" Tanner asked.

Riley groaned. Alone at the edge of the ocean, the boys sat down in the sand and opened up their bags.

"Cripes, no wonder this thing was so heavy!" Donovan declared, "I've got a freakin' kitchen in here! Stove, frying pan, cutlery..."

"Small propane canister. Water bottles. First Aid kit."

"How long are they expecting us to rough it like this?"

"Good gawd, we've got enough in here to last us a week!"

"Dried fruits and vegetables. Tent. How far are we going?"

"I don't know, but the sooner we get started, the sooner we

get finished," Tanner said. He zipped up his pack and threw it back over his shoulder.

The boys looked at one another before sliding down the dunes to the water.

"Okay Roy, that's the last smoke machine. This'll give 'em one hell of a fog. We've got water towers and for the finale, the 'Wall of Fire'."

Warren and Roy sat back to admire their handiwork. Roy's work trailer was almost empty. Except for a few well-worn paths with the ATV trailer, the forest was already starting to cover over the activity of the obstacle set-up.

"It's just like you said, Warren, the forest is hiding everything!"

"That was my only worry, that the kids would be able to see all the equipment. It will be a far more realistic challenge if they can't see what they're dealing with."

"Awesome. Are the Scuba tanks ready?"

"Yeah, but don't you think that's a bit risky?"

"A bit, but Riley and Tanner have experience. They can buddy up with Donovan...and we'll be here to make sure it's all safe."

"Okay. Then we're set."

"I'm stoked!"

"Hey, Warren. Kids say that."

"Right."

"But hey, me too. This is gonna be awesome."

"Okay, great. They should have a good catch of clams by now. Let's send them on their way."

"Do you hear that?" Riley asked.

"Hear what?" Donovan froze. He heard it too. In between the gentle lapping of waves at the edge of the beach, a faint, digital noise broke the natural soundscape.

"Sounds unusual. Not like any cell phone I know," Tanner said.

The boys walked a small pace from their position before the sound intensified. Donovan crept behind his friends and trained his ear to the sand. His head jerked this way and that before he fell to his knees. His hands tore into the sand, frantically digging. In no time he found the source of the noise.

"Hmm. That's no cell phone."

"Is it a pager?"

"I don't know. I've never seen one. There seems to be a message."

Donovan fumbled at some buttons and illuminated the tiny LED screen. A message scrolled across the screen.

"Once you have completed task 1, continue upriver."

"How do we know if we've completed task 1?"

"How big is our catch?"

"I dunno, maybe enough to live off of for a meal or two."

"Okay then, let's move on."

"Y'know, we were told we weren't allowed to bring a lot with us."

"Maybe we have to trade what we've caught for what we need?" Tanner offered.

"Isn't it illegal to catch shellfish?" Donovan inquired.

"Hmm, maybe. I'm not sure what our next objective is but I'm sure we'll figure it out."

The boys got in the canoe and eased it into the river. Calm and inviting, the glint of sun tickled the surface. It wasn't long before the incoming tide was propelling their craft farther upriver.

Donovan perked up, "Hey guys, we're about an hour away from high tide. I think our dads must've planned it this way."

"Was there a tide chart in the kit they gave us?" Tanner asked.

"Oh yeah, we should give ourselves a good look at that, shouldn't we?" Riley asked.

"I say we keep going first. We've just started paddling and it feels like the tide is in our favour. Might as well use it while we can."

Their paddles dug into the water, churning the surface. The canoe cruised through the water at a steady pace. Each boy alternated their effort so as to not tire quickly. The solitude seemed to hold them like a spell. Little was said for the first part of the voyage.

Without paying too much attention to the goings on around them, they barely noticed the normally heavy motorboat traffic had all but ceased. There were no waves rocking the side of the boat and no grinding motors to break up the silence. Even for a weekday at the end of summer, the lack of activity was noticeable.

"Wow, it's a nice quiet day, isn't it?" Tanner observed.

"Kinda strange for a beautiful summer day...?" Donovan said.

"Hey, yeah, the river should be rocking right now," Riley commented.

As the boys turned a corner, a slowing procession of boats were camped close to Rocky Point Warf. The sister town to Whispering Cove, Rocky Point Wharf was all glitz and entertainment. Teen-agers and young adults populated the boardwalk at all hours. Amusement rides, video arcades, bars, restaurants and shops lined the main street. Much to his surprise, it wasn't as rough as Riley had been led to believe, "some underbelly," he muttered.

"This must be the first checkpoint," Tanner said.

The boats that clogged the wharf, normally brimming with activity, were empty. Not a single person could be seen. The market and shops that dotted the boardwalk were noticeably quiet. There was no music and no conversation.

"Alright, this is spooky. It's like a ghost town up there," Tanner remarked.

"Maybe this is part of it. Maybe it's a big surprise," Donovan wondered.

Tanner and Riley looked at him quizzically.

"If the authorities got wind of what was going on, they'd probably haul us off to child services," Riley deducted.

"Whatever is going on, it has nothing to do with us," Tanner agreed.

It was easy to navigate past the gathered boats and look for a place to wander ashore. They skipped past the pier and looked for a place to stop and tie up their vessel. They located a small scrap of dirt in front of the break wall.

Just as they stepped out of the canoe, a low grumble shook the ground.

Riley was about to haul up the canoe when Tanner stopped him.

"Wait. That felt like a tremor of some kind."

As the boys looked up from the water toward the street, their world was completely shuttered. A massive black dump truck blocked their view of the road.

"Well, now we know what made the wharf shake," Riley mused. He pulled the canoe up the soggy clay and tied it off.

Almost as soon as the truck passed, it made an abrupt stop

and sat, idling. Over the din of the rumbling motor, the sounds of voices and commotion could be heard.

"We'd better go see what's going on," Tanner said.

"Are you sure? Shouldn't we stick to the schedule, y'know coast the tide upriver some more before taking a break?" Donovan suggested.

Tanner looked to his friend. "I don't know what Dad had in mind with this challenge, but to ignore everything until we get there kind of defeats the purpose, don't you think? Anyway, it's worth looking into. If they want to know where we are, I'm sure they've planted something amongst all this baggage to track our progress."

"It's just that you've got a nose for trouble, Tanner. Don't you remember what your dad said? We shouldn't do this," Donovan objected. Riley looked over his shoulder and clambered up the rocks ahead of Tanner.

"Do what? Get out of our canoe to take a walk on the street?" Tanner reasoned, "It'll do us some good."

The streets were filled to overflowing. The massive dump truck that shook the streets sat in the middle of the road and sputtered with quiet fury. The ratting diesel engine growled down at the milling people who stood in its path. Large picket signs leaped and jerked in front of the cabin window. From the passenger side, a man leaned out the window, a bullhorn in his hand.

As he was about to speak, the crowd rose up to drown out his voice. He retreated into his truck, locked the doors and rolled up the windows.

At the front of the throng, a small group of young men, encouraged by the energy of the crowd, turned aggressive. They dropped their signs and climbed up the side of the truck. They started to bang on the doors and windows. The driver turned this way and that, unsure what to do.

The boys watched until the faint wail of sirens started to approach. The crowd noticed, but did not budge. Two more dump trucks stopped behind the first, now surrounded by the crowd.

From behind the crowd, a few scattered teenagers ran up and hurled rocks at the truck. The banging on the windows and doors got stronger and more insistent. Helpless, the driver ducked out of view.

The wailing sirens grew louder until a squad of police cars screeched up beside the truck and skidded to a stop. Chanting, yelling, screaming, the crowd would not let the trucks pass through them.

In the midst of the chaos, Tanner spotted a dark-haired Mi'kmaq boy the same age as himself. He was bending down to pick up a rock but paused. The crowd was starting to crumble. Wafts of smoke were starting to drift up at their feet. Blinded, flailing wildly, those at the front stumbled away from the confrontation. Others started to turn and run. People toppled and fell. Pandemonium started to sweep over the ranks. The line of action slowly marched toward the dark-haired boy. The boy looked around and recognized no one. He froze. Not sure if he should stay. Not sure if he should run. Tanner saw the panic in the boy's eye. He waved frantically and called out to the lad. He yelled as loud as he could, but the roar from the crowd drowned it out. From up ahead, Tanner could see the mob careening backwards. More people fell in the panic. And that panic was aiming straight toward the dark-haired Mi'kmaq boy frozen with fear. Acting first, Tanner plunged into the chaos. As Tanner stumbled through the crowd, it started to disband.

When he reached the lad he wasted no time. He grabbed the kid by the arm and pulled him away from the bedlam. Unsure what was happening, the boy followed Tanner until all the boys were plunging down the hill toward the canoe.

As the streets erupted in mayhem, the boys, now including a fourth, pushed quickly away from shore. None of them said anything until they were safely away from the confusion.

More smoke and yelling clouded the wharf. The farther they drifted away, the less the boys could make out any resolution to the confrontation. Only when the gently lapping waves recalled their attention did they realize their jaws were clenched with tension. Tanner let out a deep breath and spoke.

"Hi, I'm Tanner."

"I'm Kim," said the boy.

"I've never seen anything like that. What was going on?" Donovan asked as the boat cruised out into the channel.

"It was a protest. French, English, Mi'kmaq. The whole town," Kim responded.

"Protesting what?" Riley asked.

"You haven't heard? The gas company's invading our land!" Kim thundered. He waved his arms around, including all of them and the surrounding wilderness.

"Oh, right," Donovan said, "I did hear, but I didn't think anything of it."

"Of course, no one expected this. I don't know why the trucks were there. They haven't been approved yet," Kim said.

"Then why were they rumbling through town?" Tanner asked.

The boys looked at one another, an answer eluding them.

"Well, I guess we better get paddling. Our dads will be waiting for us," Donovan said and reached for an oar.

"Waiting for you?" Kim asked.

"Yeah, it's kind of a long story." Tanner shrugged.

Kim looked at them as they drifted along in the waves. Away from town, Tanner recalled the story behind their present adventure.

"So it's all because you went on a joyride without brakes and tore up some old lady's lawn?" Kim said incredulously. "They decided to punish you by making you canoe by yourselves up to the end of the River of Fire? I wish I could be so lucky."

"So *lucky*?" replied Riley.

"Yeah, so lucky. D'you think this happens all the time?" Kim answered. "All three of your dads would do all of this for you?"

The other three straightened up a bit. The canoe fell silent for a moment.

"Two for sure. We're not sure about Marshal's dad. He's probably cutting a deal with the devil somewhere," Riley said.

"He's here. I know it." Donovan looked at his backpack. He nudged the side of it until he felt the familiar outline of a plastic device, small enough to fit in his hand. "How else do you think we got this map? It will take us to the portage...."

"Portage? That's nothing but a legend," Kim answered back.

"We know that," Riley blurted.

"Sure. We know that and how to give respect," Tanner said.

"So you know about Glooscap?" Kim retorted.

"We know OF him," Riley said with confidence.

"Does that mean you're going to find his wigwam? Hey, maybe this is his canoe," Kim teased.

"Ha ha, very funny. He's a god isn't he, what would he need a canoe for?"

"He's a spirit. He watches over the Mi'kmaq land. Be good to him and he'll be good to you," Kim said.

"Really?"

"Meh, something like that. Hey, can you drop me off here? This is all good fun and everything, but I better get home. Make sure you honk when you float past, that way I'll be sure to wave when you drift by."

The boys paddled back to shore, safely away from town and prying eyes.

"Look us up on Facebook, Kim," Tanner hollered after the boy as he scrambled up the riverbank.

As the boys pointed their boat upriver, Tanner turned to his friends, "I sure hope Dad doesn't have our itinerary timed by the second."

6

A Rumble in the Forest

"They shouldn't be taking this long," Warren said and paced. "At this rate it'll be nightfall before they approach the first obstacle!"

"Hopefully they have the good sense to stop and camp before any of that happens," Roy said.

"I hope so too," Warren echoed.

"Anyway, there isn't much we can do." Roy surrendered.

"Sure there is," a voice piped behind them. Warren and Roy turned to look at a short, bald, bespectacled man, clad in a tailor-made suit. Everything about the man was purposeful: his dress, his speech, his mannerisms. He entered every social interaction as though he was the smartest person in the room. Roy had a hard time holding in his contempt.

"Marshal," Roy said coldly, and gripped his hand to shake it.

"You been practicing your grip Roy, sheesh," Marshal said when the men released. He shook his hand and blew some air on it. "I'm kidding." He continued, "The boys have been waylaid. The circumstances are exceptional."

He casually reached into his leather office bag. He rummaged around before pulling out a thin, rectangular item. Stencilled neatly in a corner were the words: **Marshal Caine Enterprises**. The case housed the most recent tablet technology. With calm precision, Marshal unfurled the cover. The gleaming new tablet, which looked like it just came from the store, sprang to life.

Linked to a program neither Roy or Warren had ever heard of, Marshal was able to know the exact point along the river where the boys were located. Warren and Roy looked at one another, immediately suspicious: How could his information be so accurate and current?

"If you bothered to pay attention, you'd know a demonstration led to a riot in Rocky Point Wharf," Marshal continued.

"Say what!?!"

"We weren't paying attention because we were too busy setting everything up."

"Well, it's no big deal. They're fine. In fact, no one was injured during the event."

"Thank gawd for that," Warren said and heaved out a deep breath.

"But their exact timing saw them approach town just as tension escalated," Marshal concluded.

"I just hope they didn't get involved in any way," Roy said.

"It looks like they're past it now but I don't think they'll make it to your first challenge until tomorrow morning. Do they have enough provisions to last the night?" Marshal said.

"We made sure they were equipped," Warren responded.

"Equipped with...?"

"Camping gear. Tent. Propane stove. Sleeping bags," Roy said.

"What about food?" Marshal asked.

"Part of the challenge was for them to dig their own clams before departure," Warren said.

Marshal shot them a look of extreme concern, "Are the clams safe? Do any of the boys have allergies? Do they have an Epi-pen? Do they know how to use it?"

His response was rapid-fire, his voice controlled. It wasn't meant to alarm. Marshal was accustomed to thinking of the worst-case scenario and planning accordingly. In so responding, his training was to always keep his quarry off-guard during a negotiation. He never knew when to surrender his business persona.

"Er, I'm not sure," Warren stammered.

Roy, gear head though he was, had more than his fair share of verbal confrontations and was able to hold his own.

"They have an emergency kit. An epi-pen is standard in those kits," he said, trying his best to remain calm. "The clams are fine if they're cooked. There is only one reason for the warning signs for clam digging. It's so the tourists don't get sick. My son is acclimated to having seafood in his diet, as is Tanner. We dig our own clams and prepare them accordingly."

"But Donovan hasn't!" Marshal exclaimed and reached into his bag for his phone, "we need to abort—"

Roy reached over and stopped Marshal from making a call.

"Yes he has," Roy whispered.

It was Marshal's turn at surprise. His mouth fell open. He searched his database of memory. When had it happened? And more importantly, how did Roy know about it and he didn't?

Roy wanted badly to cherish the moment when he caught the great Marshal Caine by surprise. The moment he got the upper hand and knew something his nemesis didn't.

"At my house. A few times now. He loves them. He helped me cook them and can them. You must have been away."

The silence was thick for a minute as Marshal searched for

an answer.

"And they have other dried goods. Berries, nuts, water treatment tablets and water bottles," Warren interjected.

"Why didn't he tell me? Why didn't he say anything?" Marshal asked the other dads. Warren and Roy both shrugged.

"They're getting older and there's going to be a lot more they're not going to tell us," Warren said.

It was taking Marshal some time to reconcile with the revelation that his son was starting to live a life of his own making. A life Marshal would never completely share. He took a deep breath and composed himself.

"Now, if you could explain to me what you have set up here and I'll see where I can help."

"Can you believe what Kim said?" Riley spouted.

"Come on guys, there's no way. I mean, a protective spirit that watches over the entire river? Seriously," Donovan said.

The three of them chuckled. A nervousness hung in the air.

"Riley, can you help me with this tent? I can't seem to figure it out," Donovan said. Riley nudged Tanner in the ribs and pointed at Donovan. The stout lad held the tent up before rotating it around in his hands. He looked down at the box then back to the crumpled mess in front of him. Donovan dug into the box and pulled out the instructions. The paper unfurled before him. It was like trying to learn a new language.

"Here, let me help," Riley said and grabbed a corner of the tent. Donovan ditched the instructions and followed the lead of his friend.

"You got the corner?" Riley called and winked at Tanner.

"I think so," Donovan answered and double-checked.

At that moment Riley tugged at the tent, toppling Donovan along with it.

"Hey, cut it out Riley," Donovan said and scrambled to his feet. He was about to walk over and take a shove at his friend when he slipped on a rock. His arms flailed. Riley grabbed his ribs and started to laugh. Frustrated at the shenanigans, Tanner stood up and extended the end of a tent pole to help his friend.

Just as Donovan was about to grab it, Tanner lost his balance and poked the stick into Donovan. Falling, flailing and swinging his arms, Donovan searched for anything to arrest his momentum. Riley, not quite out of reach, fell into the mess. All three boys toppled into a heap.

"You stupid," Donovan yelled and pushed back at Tanner. What was once fun and jokes quickly turned. The boys jostled with one another. Pushing, shoving and retaliating.

"Why did you have to poke at me like that!"

"It was an accident. I was trying to help."

"Do you call that trying to help?"

"Better than you did, pulling him off balance like that."

"Snicker. Snicker. Usually you read the instructions BEFORE you go camping."

"Oh you are SUCH an ass!"

The boys stopped when they heard the familiar sharp crack of plastic colliding with rock. It was a sound they knew quite well. Crisp but hollow. The first bounce was loud. The others more frequent but less bold. The movement caught all of their attention. The plastic was palm-sized, black and shiny. A sight many of them knew all to well. The tiny smartphone loped off the rock. In desperate awe, the boys watched dumbstruck, as it rolled and rocked this way and that down the slope before gurgling in the water.

After it settled all three got up and dove down to look at the unit. A few bubbles escaped from the back and drifted to the surface. The LCD screen remained lit for a brief moment before snuffing itself out.

"Awww crap!" Donovan said.

"You cheater!" Riley thundered and shoved Donovan to help himself stand up.

"What, come on! Riley, how do you think we got where we are?" Donovan countered. Still on the ground, he brought his legs and hands up to defend himself. Riley stepped back but continued to tower over his friend.

"Oh please! It's a river. It's big. There's only one way to go. Here, just look at this map!" Riley said.

Tanner scrambled to his feet and stood between his two friends, trying to make peace.

"Guys, knock it off!" Tanner interjected. He dug his hand into the cool water and scooped out the smartphone.

"If we let it dry out it might still work," Tanner said.

"Oh, so you're with him eh! Come on! We have a map and we know where we're going. We don't need that and besides we're not supposed to have it anyway," Riley continued.

"I know Riley," Tanner considered, "but that's before we paddled through a riot."

Riley thought for a moment, "That's none of our business. We don't live there. It's not our problem!"

"Just the same," Tanner said and handed the device back to Donovan, "we'll put it away and respect our Dads' wishes."

Riley stomped away in a huff. Tanner extended a hand to Donovan and helped him back to his feet.

As he passed the device into Donovan's hands the three boys

returned to setting up camp. Keeping their respective distances, each boy took ownership of a certain task. Riley unfurled the tent, Donovan set up the propane stove and Tanner gathered some rocks into a circle.

Shooting a glance to Riley, Tanner motioned to the soggy smartphone in his hands. He whispered to Donovan, "Be sure to get it dried out."

Tanner marched away from camp. Before he did he called over his shoulder, "I'm going to get some firewood!"

"I remember my first camp out," Warren said. "My dad took me to a site by the beach. I can still feel the heat of that bonfire on my cheeks."

"Eating marshmallows and hot dogs," Marshal added.

All three men chuckled at the memory.

"How old were you when camped by yourself?" Warren asked.

"Does the backyard count?" Marshal asked.

Laughter.

"I bet you were a big coward in the dark, Marshal," Roy took a dig.

"My dad always made sure I had a solution for every little problem," Marshal responded.

"Gawd, I was terrified, even though the tent was on our back deck," Warren confessed.

"Yup, me too," Roy said.

"You mean you didn't have a small arsenal to make you feel better?" Marshal dug back.

"My old man was VERY careful with his rifle. He always made sure to teach me how to respect it and treat it like the tool it is."

"Okay guys, stop it! Marshal, don't ask Roy about guns and Roy don't ask Marshal about technology. We're here for our sons, remember," Warren reminded them.

"You're right, you're right," Roy conceded, "they're probably just settling in for the night. They've had some excitement."

"Yes, more than any of us anticipated. Though I have it on good authority," Marshal absent-mindedly reached into his pocket for his smartphone, "..that they are just shy of your first obstacle."

Roy turned to look at Marshal intensely, "Wait, how could you know their exact location?"

"When I knew they wouldn't reach the first checkpoint, I decided to locate them on the satellite," Marshal shrugged.

His voice was met with silence.

"What?" Marshal said, not registering the accusing look on the other men's faces.

"This adventure is as much about us trusting our boys as them needing to prove themselves as young men. No technology! They have too much of it in their lives all the time. Hell, they're probably more scared of being away from video games and the internet for a night more than they're terrified of the dark," Warren said.

"Yeah, you're right I guess," Marshal conceded.

"They're almost men. It's more important they know how to survive on their wits and their nerve," Roy exclaimed.

"And another thing..." Warren wanted to continue.

"Okay, okay, I get it, geez," Marshal conceded.

As he finished speaking, his breath was arrested by a low rumble. A wave of energy seemed to grow out of the woods. First it was a loud thunderous roar that rattled every hair follicle on their head. Then a wave of energy overpowered them and hurled them to the ground. All three men were thrown to the dirt. By instinct, they covered their heads. The source appeared to move through the woods. Trees rippled and swayed. The ground beneath them heaved.

Moments that seemed like hours passed before the rush of energy was followed by a deafening CRACK. It was a dull sound but immensely powerful. Not sharp and crisp like thunder, but just as voluminous.

The men remained still for several minutes before Roy raised his head.

"Uh, pyrotechnics weren't supposed to happen until tomorrow."

"WHAT was that!?!" Warren said.

"I don't want to stick around to find out," Marshal said.

"You didn't bring any pyrotechnics?" Warren asked Roy.

"No, I swear. Nothing. Not so much as a firecracker. I was leaving all of that home under lock and key until we were going to use it."

"Whatever that was had to be caused by something. There might be more," Warren reasoned.

"Until we know what's going on, the boys' adventure should be put on hold. First there was a riot. Now an explosion or an earthquake or something. This is too dangerous. Marshal, with humblest apologies, technology is absolutely necessary. Is there any way we can get in touch with the boys?"

"Uh, yeah, that would be a great idea," Marshal said, still in shock. He stared straight ahead as reached into his pocket for his smartphone. He dialed the number quickly. All three men gathered around and waited to communicate with their sons.

After a few moments, Marshal pulled the phone away from his ear, disbelief spread across his face.

"Customer is unavailable," he finally said.

"We need to find them," Warren concluded.

"Okay, let's go. I'm driving," Roy barked. He grabbed his keys and tore off out of the camp.

Warren, a little behind the frenzied pace of his friend, snapped to attention and started to snuff out the fire. He was about to run after Roy when he noticed Marshal standing rooted to the ground, unable to move. Warren grabbed him by the arm and together they scrambled to find their sons.

7

The Trailer in the Woods

"Okay, that was no ordinary thunderstorm. That was close and that was serious," Tanner exclaimed.

"Think it had anything to do with the dump truck that rolled through town earlier?" Riley asked.

"I don't think it's a coincidence, assuming that noise we heard was not the result of a natural cause," Donovan said.

"Something's going down," Riley said.

"Uh huh. But where?" Tanner asked.

"Hmmph, betcha wish my smartphone worked now!" Donovan crowed.

"Sure I do. And while you guys are huffing and puffing like crazy trying to dry it out, I'm going to take a hike and try to find a house or something," Riley said.

"Wait, I think we should all go," Donovan interjected.

"Why?"

"Well, Riley, you should have a buddy go with you. But that means someone is left at camp by themselves. Not a good idea," Donovan reasoned.

"And besides, we might dry out the BlackBerry and it might not work anyway. But let's bring it. You never know. Maybe wrap it in some toilet paper or something."

Donovan set to work wrapping his BlackBerry in toilet paper. Around and around he went. He stopped for a moment as he held the wad of white in front of him. They all laughed.

"Good thing I have extra-large pockets," Donovan said and jammed the device into his pants.

"Just don't sit down or you'll fall over lopsided," Riley laughed.

"Okay guys, enough kidding around. Are we ready?" Tanner said impatiently.

Taking only essential items and then making sure the boat was fastened tight, the boys scrambled up the bank of the river.

The setting of the evening sun blitzed the forest with an intense red hue. Tanner paused for a moment.

'Could there be some substance to those native legends?' he thought to himself. He was just about to voice his thoughts when Riley broke the silence.

"Wow. Incredible! Now I know why they call it the River of Fire," Riley exclaimed into the deafening silence.

The three boys lost themselves completely in the moment. The spirit had arrested them, if even for just a brief, intense, wrinkle of time. The boys forgot where they were and what they were doing. It was as though Glooscap himself had struck a torch and placed it in the middle of the river and sent plumes of flame billowing into the sky.

But what it was really doing was calling out to them. Beckoning them. The fictional challenge that was created to test their wits and mettle had been replaced by something real and tangible.

The machine was almost on top of them before the gaze of the river spirit released them from its grip. The four-wheeler growled to a halt. As he leapt from the machine and ditched his helmet, Kim was jabbering away.

"Thank gawd you guys are okay," Kim managed to say.

"Yeah, we're fine. We're all fine," Tanner answered.

"Good. That's great. I guess it's better to be a kid alone in the woods," Kim huffed.

"What do you mean?"

"What I mean is there's an evacuation and I'm the native kid who saw you guys last. If something happened to you, I'm the first person they'd ask. Geez, it's a good thing you didn't make it much farther after you dropped me off this afternoon," Kim explained.

"Evacuation?"

"Oh yeah, I guess you don't have a radio or anything like that," Kim mumbled.

Donovan reached into his back pocket. He unfurled his smartphone from the mass of toilet paper.

"We're off the grid," Riley snickered as he looked at the crippled device.

Donovan hung his head.

"Is everyone okay at the reserve?" Tanner asked.

"Okay, like mentally undeveloped okay or okay like not consumed by a giant disaster?"

"He's funny!" Riley exclaimed.

"Sorry, I didn't mean it like that," Tanner returned.

Kim stared at Tanner for a moment. Tanner returned his gaze before Kim broke into a grin.

"I know you didn't, I'm just messing with you."

"Did you say evacuation?" Riley inquired.

"Yeah, it's kinda crazy right now. All I heard in town for the past few hours is sirens and screaming. It ain't a Saturday night, so something is out of the ordinary," Kim offered.

"How far is Harry's land from the reserve?" Tanner asked.

"Harry who? Eaglesmith?" Kim answered.

"You know him?"

"He was my uncle."

"Was?"

"It's complicated. Okay, I found you guys, now I think you should come with me."

"Go with you?"

"Remember the part where we just talked about an evacuation and me being the last one to know your whereabouts? Yeah, that kinda makes me responsible for you, and if something happens to you because of me, I'm totally screwed."

"At least you're not afraid to admit you're only here to save your own skin," Riley said.

"Y'know I could just say I went back to look for you and couldn't find you," Kim retorted.

"Guys, stop!" Tanner barked, "What about our dads?"

"Your dads? Like plural Dad? I don't have enough room on the four-wheeler," Kim said.

"They're waiting for us. They're expecting us. We should at least go see them and tell them what's going on," Tanner said.

"And I'm a taxi service now?"

"No, you don't have to do anything. I'm concerned about my dad and Marshal and Roy. They need to know we're okay. If you want to follow us to save your own skin, go ahead. But if you gave us a ride, it would speed up the process."

Tanner launched his backpack over his shoulder and strode away into the woods. Riley and Donovan looked at Kim before they trundled after him.

"Stop!" Kim called, "hop on!"

"I was hoping he was going to say that," Donovan said with a sigh of relief. He spun around quickly and climbed onto the machine. Riley wasn't far behind him.

Kim hit the throttle to rev the engine. Tanner bounded onto the ATV, jimmying with the other two boys for whatever space was available. Kim sped off down the trail.

"I thought it best if we approached from the forest," Kim said as the engine started to wind down. He pulled the ATV into a small dip in the woods. "We're close to Harry's camp," Kim said.

"We should hide the ATV. If our dads are still here, we don't want them to know how we got here," Riley suggested.

"Don't cover it too good," Tanner said. "We still need to be able to find it."

"Which way is the river?" Donovan asked.

"This way," Kim motioned. "Follow me."

Snaking their way through the thick foliage, the boys filed down through the trees.

"I hope he knows where he's going," Donovan exclaimed, "because I haven't got a clue where I am!"

"Don't worry, I've fished this river before. If he wasn't going the right way, I'd know," Riley returned.

The terrain turned and dipped. With startling abruptness, the trees came to an end. A small cliff gave way to the gently lapping river some ten feet below them.

Kim hesitated a moment, waiting for the rest of the boys to catch up. He stepped over the side and slid down the gravel to the river

Unbeknownst to them, some fifty yards upriver, a motion

sensor triggered a series of fog machines. The units sputtered to life and kicked thick, artificial fog across the river.

As Kim turned to go a little farther upriver, the gradual mists gently came into view. Riley, suspecting his father's handiwork, turned to reveal his observations to his friends. He was just about to verbalize his thoughts when the fog thickened and swallowed them in its midst.

"Okay, guys," Riley said, "let's find the machine and shut it off!"

But somehow the forest swallowed his words the way the fog had swallowed his friends and he had no way of knowing if his voice was heard.

"Keep walking along the shore. There should be plenty of ground to walk on, as long as the tide is low," Kim said, wondering if he too was heard.

Riley hung back from the last point he'd seen the rest of his friends. To him it seemed as though they had disappeared. It didn't make any sense for him to follow along to be just as blind.

With the trees and the wind, the fog must be collecting down the river like a channel, he thought to himself before scrambling up the bank to the top of the cliff.

"Well," he said as wafts of smoke broke near him, "some visibility is better than no visibility."

Riley worked his way slowly through the forest. Moving deliberately, he did his best to try and keep the edge of the thick fog near enough to know his approximation to the river.

"Riley!" Tanner exclaimed, "can you hear me?"

"Yes!" Riley shouted as loud as he could. To Tanner it was just a faint whisper that he strained to hear.

"How do you think they knew we were coming?"

65

The response was muffled and eventually swallowed by the fog. Tanner shrugged his shoulders before trying another tack.

"Hey Kim, my feet are starting to get wet. Do you know if the tide is coming in?" he asked.

He paused. Deafening silence. The fog affected his hearing as much as his sight. He reached out his hands to touch it. He felt eerily paralyzed. He needed to know there was some sense he could trust. He waved his hands in front of him. Small wafts of fog curled around his hand and clung to him.

"Oh no, we should have stayed together," he muttered aloud.

He fidgeted for a moment, unsure what to do. The damp around his feet started to seep into his boots. He turned to head back in the direction he came and walked directly into something solid.

"Ouch!" two voices shrieked in unison.

As Tanner crumpled to the earth, somebody stumbled and fell on top of him. Donovan, and then a second person, added to the weight.

"Riley, is that you?" Donovan said fumbling around in the fog.

"Aw, guys, can you get off me?" Tanner begged.

The boys scrambled to their feet, grumbling all the way.

"Hey, wait, the fog is breaking up," Kim said.

"Guess there was only so much formula," Donovan guessed.

"I suppose so. Alright, let's go find Riley," Tanner said.

"I'm right here, guys. I didn't know you had time to stop and have a cuddle," from the top of the bluff Riley looked down at his friends. "Come on, I unplugged the machines. Let's get going." He reached out to help his friends climb up the slope.

The boys trudged single file through the forest. Tanner couldn't keep his inquisitive mind silent. When he took a moment to look around he realized not one of his friends was saying anything. Maybe if he asked his questions out loud they might discover something.

"Kim, do you have any idea what caused the earthquake we heard earlier?"

"I don't know too much. Honestly. Some things are just rumours. Stories around town," Kim replied.

"What do you mean?"

"A company wants to open a big mine here. There's been lots of activity from people that come from away. Exploration. Tests looking for this and that. Oil. Gas. Gold. Uranium. Copper. Anything and everything. And promises to make us all rich."

"But it's definitely something?" Tanner asked.

"Very much so. Some people want it and some people don't. Some people think we should do everything we can to open our doors and make some money," Kim said and stopped. "Where did that come from?"

With no further explanation Kim took off on a trot through the woods. The rest of the boys followed.

"Hey guys, wait," Riley called, "I think it's my dad's trailer."

8

Unreliable Network

Nestled in the woods, a modest tow-behind trailer sat in solitude amongst the canopy of green and forest. A padlock barred the doors. The boys stood and stared a moment as Riley walked around the trailer. He reached up under the body. Finding nothing, he continued along. Seeing what he was up to, the rest of the boys caught on and spread out looking for the same: a key. Everyone except Tanner. He spun the body of the lock away from the loop and was met with no resistance.

"They dummy locked them," Tanner called to Riley.

When it became obvious the trailer had been opened by someone else, Riley didn't break off his search right away. If he knew his stepdad like he thought he did, there might be other secret tools stashed away. Finding nothing, he walked into a conversation the other boys were having at the back door.

"Okay, so we opened it, now what?" Kim asked.

"Roy!" Donovan stuck his head in the back and yelled into the trailer. His voice echoed off the walls.

"They could still be out in the forest, setting obstacles," Tanner offered.

"Seems pretty obvious to me they aren't here," Kim concluded.

"A few hours ago, we heard a rumble in the woods," said Riley. "Nobody really knows what it was, but we all agree it wasn't natural. We show up here and all three dads are nowhere to be found. My stepdad used to be a special effects guy in LA. He's got some serious stuff in his arsenal that's probably not legal."

"Did anybody else know that?" Tanner asked.

"Come on, Tanner, do you think Dad had a big neon sign: 'Hey, illegal fireworks here!'?"

"What about Harry?" Donovan asked and fixed his eyes on Kim. "If Harry owns the camp, then Harry must've known what they were planning."

"Maybe they went to find you," Kim responded, "without bringing modern technology. Gee, that was smart."

"They had technology, remember?" Donovan gestured to the decrepit phone in his pocket.

"Riley, you must know your dad's trailer. Do you think you'd be able to tell if anything is missing?" Tanner suggested.

"If it were packed, maybe. I'm sure his gear is strung out all over Acadia by now."

As Tanner thought about the problem, Riley strode up the centre of the trailer. He didn't bother to look too far. The walls were lined with shelving that was noticeably empty. The rest of the boys followed. Being unfamiliar with the gear didn't prevent them from being curious about the trinkets and connectors and gack that still lingered.

Donovan and Kim were both looking high and low, occasionally losing themselves in the strange equipment. Tanner focused on the labels and descriptions. He muttered as he went, hoping perhaps a word might trigger a clue. Riley walked to the front. A small office greeted him.

Tanner shuffled along the aisle. He noticed some words written along the facing of the shelving. He read them loud enough for Riley to hear.

"Caps. Couplings. Connectors. Fire Bar. Propane Valves. Water Manifold."

"Wait!" Riley called.

"What? What word?"

"Propane Valves."

"Okay."

Riley picked up something from the office and walked back into the trailer.

"That's a walkie-talkie," Donovan observed.

"Yeah, Dad always told me to NEVER have a walkie turned on when using explosives. I saw him do a fireball once. Maybe that caused the earthquake!"

"Do you think they had an accident?" Tanner mused before the gravity of the statement caught his attention. The trailer filled with silence.

The boys considered the possibility that something might have happened to their fathers while they were preparing the obstacle course. Riley's hand clenched for a moment. They were about to move to comfort one another but stopped immediately when a 'blip' echoed around them.

"It was the walkie," Kim exclaimed.

All eyes fixated on Riley's hand. Riley pulled the walkie to his mouth.

"Uh. Uh. Hello? Dad?"

Silence.

"Guess it was noth—" and Riley stopped short again as the walkie gave another beep.

"How many walkie talkies does your dad have?" Tanner

asked.

"Two more besides this one, I think," Riley responded as the walkie made another beep. The boys started to talk over it as the speaker continued spitting out intermittent noise.

"Aww man!" Donovan lamented at the smartphone in his hands. "Why did we have to drop this stupid thing in the river? Now it's useless! If it was working, I might be able to figure out where they are right now! I could pinpoint them with a few swipes of the screen!"

"No, you couldn't," Kim countered.

"Sure I could. It's easy," Donovan scoffed.

"You need a network first. We're off the grid here."

"How do you know?"

"Check it out," Kim said and held up his phone. "Searching for network."

"You mean there's no service? No wireless? How is that even possible?"

"We're in the woods. Miles from civilization, you can't expect the internet out here."

Disappointment spread across the boys' faces. The one source of information they could rely on to answer any question they might have was inaccessible.

"This is getting us nowhere. It's obvious they're not here. And they have no way of getting in touch with us. We should spread out to try and find them," Riley suggested.

"I know my Dad's gear better than any of us. I know what to look for and I'll be able to find it in the woods. If they're still making obstacles, I'll be able to find them."

"They might have been caught up in the evacuation," Kim offered.

"But they would have been able to leave us a note or something like that," Donovan countered. "Or alert the authorities about us. And there's nothing here. They either don't know anything about the evacuation..."

"...Or they didn't get evacuated," Tanner finished.

"What does that mean?"

"How close is Harry Eaglesmith to these miners?"

"What, like literally?"

"Sure, let's start there. Is where we're standing right now close to the site?" Tanner asked.

"Yeah, I think so."

"Then we should look there."

"But the miners aren't supposed to be doing anything here," Kim continued. There's an injunction in place ..."

"Injunction?" Riley asked.

"It's an order to stop...isn't it?" Tanner said.

"Sounds to me like everything points to the mining company," Donovan remarked.

"I don't like it. I don't like it. I don't like it," Tanner threw his arms in the air and tousled his hair. The other boys slumped back.

"Now what are we supposed to do?" Donovan finally asked. "We have no means of communication."

"Except the walkie-talkie," Riley pointed out. He pulled the device off of his belt buckle and looked at it. He flipped the dial, calling "Dad" and waiting after each turn. He passed through every channel. "Nothing." He hung his head and put the walkie on a shelf.

"What's that red dot?" Tanner asked and stared at the small LED light. The light seemed to flicker. Tanner seized the walkie and flipped through each of the channels.

"When I try every channel, there's no light. Except channel

9. And look, it's flickering. It goes on and then off."

"Does that mean anything?" Donovan asked.

"Didn't you guys go to Scouts? That looks like a code," Kim explained.

"Morse Code?" Riley asked.

"Okay, does anyone know Morse Code?"

"Do you really think even if I was in something as lame as the Scouts," Riley turned to Kim and smirked, "that I would remember Morse Code?"

"There's gotta be an app for that," Tanner commented.

"Yeah, but our phone's dead, remember?" Donovan said.

"What about a book or something? Maybe my dad has something in the office," Riley said.

"Good idea. Wait, we can't all do the same thing. Riley, why don't you go find your Dad's gear? Donovan should stay here and look in the office for a book on Morse Code. Since Kim knows these woods, maybe the two of us can find the mining site and see if our dad's are there."

The boys froze a moment. Stunned. They stared at Tanner. They were remembering a different boy. The one they'd known all their lives. The one who cried when he fell and scraped his arms and knees. The one who was afraid of bugs, the dark, and...girls. This was someone completely different.

"Uh, that is unless somebody else has a better idea," Tanner offered, suddenly a little self-conscious.

The boys looked at one another for an instant. They hadn't been spoken to in such a forceful fashion before by one of their own. Riley was the first to break the tension.

"Okay, I've got work to do," Riley said and ran out of the trailer. Tanner strode out of the trailer with Kim. Kim followed behind before overtaking Tanner as the two of them set off into the woods.

Donovan sat in a rickety chair and spotted a wooden box. He dumped out its contents before noticing another walkie. He picked it up and checked it over. He was about to toss it into a corner when a thought popped into his head. *Maybe the battery is dead.*

He searched around for a few moments, looking for a charger. A poster sat on the desk. "Say No to Industrial Mining. Save our Natural Habitat." He read through the fine print.

"Hmm," Donovan said aloud, "was Riley's dad a protester?"

He scanned the poster until the names of people and companies leapt from the page: The White Wizard of Acadia Mining Company CEO John Gerryston. He carried the poster out of the office and cleared space on a work bench to lay it out. He set the walkie beside it. He thought it best to remove the vital clues and collect them together in one space. At his feet, a small heating fan sprang to life, startling him. He bent down to turn it off before inspiration took hold. From his back pocket, he unfurled the crippled smartphone from the toilet paper. Pulling the gadget apart, he separated the battery from the unit. A safe distance from the small heater, he set the phone down, determined to see it reactivated.

"We won't get anywhere if we can't communicate with the outside world. I bet the smartphone will find a network before that old fossil will be of any use!" Donovan declared as he shook the walkie. He placed it on the bench and took a deep breath.

"Now, there must be something in here we can use," he said before continuing his investigation.

Tanner and Kim marched silently through the woods. Tanner

was trying his hardest to concentrate on points of interest or other indicators, but one tree looked exactly like another. He was quickly losing hope and momentum. It was a few moments before Kim noticed he didn't hear any footsteps following his own. He stopped. Tanner was gazing around, concentrating and straining to suck every piece of the forest into his memory.

"You'll never remember everything!" Kim called as he headed towards Tanner.

"It's part of your people to know exactly where you are at all times isn't it?" Tanner asked.

"We're still people, too. I've never been this far away from the river or the road. But my father taught me something," Kim said. He reached for the first small twig that came into his view. With both hands, he snapped the small branch and let it dangle at the side of the tree. He snapped three more. When one broke off completely, he took the foliage and wove it through a limb.

"There. Every few steps or so, we'll keep doing that and we'll be able to retrace our steps. Do you really think that just because I'm Mi'kmaq I know these woods by some spiritual guide? Come on," Kim said and laughed.

In a clearing in the woods, Riley happened along an orange extension cord meandering along the forest floor. Up and over ferns, around moss covered sandstone tickling out of the earth, Riley followed.

Too bad, Riley thought to himself. *I bet Dad was having a blast working at his old job again.*

Recessed into the woods, away from the river that now winked through the tree trunks, Riley spotted the beachhead of the first obstacle. Or so he thought.

He approached the stacked mass of hoses and valves that, in a different context might be considered abstract art.

"This is probably a wall of water that he had set up. Okay, so if I follow the hoses I can bet that one of them goes off into the river," Riley determined. He observed the pile once again, closed his eyes and selected one of the valves.

"I'll follow this one," he said and started to walk away from the pile. He pulled it up as he walked along. Occasionally he would stop to see where the hose was leading, but quickly lost hope. Except for what he was holding in his hands, the rest of the channel was swallowed up by the forest.

Growing frustrated, Riley retreated to the valve tree. He pulled the hose off to make sure he didn't follow the same one.

"Only eight more to go," he muttered under his breath. He stood up and followed another hose that snaked deep into the woods.

In the trailer, Donovan wrote down a few notes. If he didn't know any better, he would have sworn that Roy Jones used his trailer as his personal library. Donovan gazed at the titles that lined the shelves: Metallurgy. Principles in Special Effects. Welding. Fire propulsion. Handbooks. Code Books. Two full shelving units filled the office. As Donovan scanned over the covers, his first observation was all of the books had been well-used.

He pulled the first book from the shelf and took it down. He flipped through the pages, stopping at the table of contents.

"No Morse Code," he said. He reached for the second book,

his eyes drifting to the small paperback in the middle of the second row.

He stuffed one book back, pulled out the next and rifled through the pages. Halfway through the first row, he couldn't help himself.

"*Your Disaster Survival Guide,*" he read aloud. He tugged at the small paperback. As he did a worn, folded piece of paper fell out between it and the other book. The newsprint was faded slightly. Smudged. He unfolded it and noticed bold handwriting at the bottom: *CAN'T CONFIRM!* Donovan's eyes widened as he noticed the headline of the article:

Eco-Terrorists Sabotage Pipeline

"Can't confirm? What can't he confirm?"

Donovan placed the article down on the desk before he noticed a word was underlined in the article:

Big Six Corporate Holdings Inc.

He continued to read the article until he stumbled across an image that made his eyes bulge: a square-jawed man with flowing silver hair. Even in the picture, the man's gaze was intense and hypnotizing. Underneath the photo was the caption: company spokesperson John Gerryston.

"*John Gerryston?*" Donovan thought to himself. He held the article in his hand and looked at the poster on the bench. He picked up the poster and stared at the words "White Wizard of Acadia CEO John Gerryston."

He held the article in one hand and the poster in the other and thought out loud, "*Is it the same guy?*"

His search took on a new sense of urgency. He pitched the article onto the bench and tore through the shelving. He pulled out each book as fast as he could and held the pages open and shook the contents. Another folded newspaper drifted to the floor, then another. Intermittent pages and newsprint fluttered out. When he was finished, he gathered up the information, along with the survival guidebook, and laid them out on the bench.

He opened the folded pages one by one.

"Grocery list" Donovan read, crumpling the page and tossing it into the garbage.

"Equipment list. Blueprint. Getting warmer," he read aloud.

"Memorandum of understanding, White Wizard. Okay, that's two articles that mention the White Wizard," he took the page and set it with the other relevant information.

"Police turn back protesters at Lone Pine Engineering site," he said aloud. He scanned the rest of the article looking for any mention of John Gerryston or White Wizard. He grumbled when he saw nothing. He set the paper down and picked up another.

"Stocks tumble on earnings report. Coniferous Enterprises. Looks like it's another mining company. But so what, Roy might be a shareholder," Donovan stepped back. He shook his head and walked away.

On the bench, the red light continued to blink short staccato bursts followed by long pauses.

Donovan sat, his head bowed between his knees. He clasped his hands behind his head. He went over the clippings. None of it made sense to him. The articles seemed random. Disjointed. If only he had internet access, he could take a lead and uncover a little more. He exhaled deeply. Unsure what to do, he looked over his shoulder and noticed he hadn't touched the survival book.

"Oh well, nothing to lose," he said aloud and gained his feet. He flipped through the pages before stumbling onto a chart. Dashes and dots. He picked up the walkie and stared at the blinking light. Thinking quickly, he tore into the office, looking for a pen. With great intensity he wrote down the message. The light went out.

"SOS. Danger."

"More, you need to tell me more," Donovan said to the walkie. "Is that you, Dad? I've known Tanner my whole life. Riley I just met a few years ago. Do I really know much about him?"

A voice at the back of the trailer startled him.

"I could say I don't know much about you either," Riley commented, "but at least I know my stepdad is home every night. Can you say the same thing?"

"Cut it out Riley, I'm thinking out loud," Donovan defended.

"Yeah, well, you're implying that my stepdad is some kind of villain and he's not!" Riley thundered.

"I take it back, okay? But look at all of this," Donovan said, pointing to the bench. "He might not be a villain, but he isn't innocent, either. He was following some other protests pretty closely." He shuffled through the articles.

"But none of it connects," Riley commented as he loomed over the bench. As his mind raced, Donovan remembered the smartphone. He picked up the pieces and stitched it back together. He closed his eyes and held the power button.

With a reluctant crackle, the phone sprang to life.

"YES!" he said.

"So what, you need a network, don't you?" Riley said.

Donovan stared down at the screen. A bar sprang to attention.

"Ah ha, now we'll be able to find some answers!" Donovan laughed triumphantly as he held the device in front of Riley.

"Check again."

Donovan turned the screen back. His friend was right. The single bar flickered and went out. It blurted back to attention.

"You're back on the grid, but you're on dial-up!"

9

Strange Allies

Tanner and Kim breezed along the forest. Kim managed to stay low enough to avoid the low-hanging branches of the underbrush. Tanner, doing his best to follow, huffed in frustration at not being able to see through the thickets. They seemed to be on sort of a path. Exactly where it went and would end up, he had absolutely no clue. But as the path wore on and narrowed, he realized it was not made by humans. A claustrophobia gripped his mind. Tanner halted in his tracks. Kim continued to steam on before he realized his footsteps weren't being echoed.

He took careful note of where they were. Sharp beams of light penetrated through the woods. Though the summer days were still long, the lengthening shadows told him the sun would be setting soon. He reversed his steps and turned back toward his new friend.

"Have the winds grabbed you?" Kim asked as he noticed that Tanner seemed to be rooted like the endless tree canopy that engulfed them.

"Maybe. It's weird, I just had this really strange... I don't know....It was like tunnel vision. Everything around me turned and closed the path. Almost like the trees were starting to block my way."

Kim sized up his new friend. Though he considered himself an expert of the woods, even he had to admit he'd rarely heard anyone mention something so strange. And the last person to mention such a thing was himself. When he walked the woods, it was to a nearby fishing hole where the underbrush was too thick to take the four-wheeler. The machine was never too far away. He also sensed through his own intuition that Tanner was neither scared nor joking. Kim didn't know how to react.

"You keep saying things like that and we Mi'kmaq are gonna start talking funny about you," Kim responded. "It's starting to get late. I thought it wasn't far away but I guess it's a little further than I anticipated. Let's head back to the trailer and see if Donovan found anything."

It didn't surprise Donovan that the walkie should go silent. Wherever and whatever circumstances his father was in, it was doubtful that sending detailed information would be possible. The info he had would have to be enough for further research. If he could get the smartphone to cooperate, he might be able to piece together the snippets of information on the bench. They were related in some way, and Donovan was certain he could piece together the various connections.

"Every company. Every business and corporation have their own internal databases," his father had told him once. "They are the very brains of how they're run. Some operations have the luxury of being transparent. Others not so much," Marshal had said. "But no matter how a company is received on the outside, someone on the board of directors has full knowledge of what they're doing and how they're doing it. There's always someone who has the final say. But, more importantly, whether good or bad, there is always a blueprint that leads to those decisions."

Like most kids whose father worked on the road, Donovan had a passing interest in his affairs. Marshal would share tidbits of what he did with his son almost like he wanted Donovan to understand his world. Try as he might, Donovan only vaguely grasped what that world entailed.

"I'm a consultant," Marshal would say at social gatherings. "I work in the financial sector."

Donovan would try to hold his interest, drawn, as always, to the constant attention Marshal showed his smartphone.

"Excuse me, I have to take this," he would say before drifting into another room for privacy. Marshal never minded when Donovan followed. After all, even if he knew his business, who could he share it with and why would they care? So even though he didn't completely understand his fathers' profession, Donovan gained valuable insight into how to unlock doors to exclusive information.

And when his father was away to a far-flung place on a business excursion, it should only stand to reason that, left alone without a strong male hand, he should begin to test the scope of his knowledge.

Gaming was Donovan's primary fixation. He would find programming loopholes to improve his gaming experience. What was more fun than breezing through a level your friends spent months trying to solve? He was stonewalled on a few occasions. Some game releases were as closely guarded as military secrets. On others, it was almost as though they handed him the path. He was starting to question who made those decisions and why.

Donovan found a back entry into the *Quest for Triumph* database through a fan forum. The contact, who eventually busted him and blocked his further efforts, was quite envious of his talents at such a young age. It wasn't long before they struck up an online friendship and shared other cyber secrets. Taking those lessons and applications into the real world, with a great deal more at stake, had so far sapped Donovan's initiative.

He started with the last piece of information: Coniferous Enterprises. He did a quick search and paired it with 'White Wizard'. He quickly found White Wizard was hired by Coniferous Enterprises to conduct exploration testing.

"Okay, so who are Coniferous Enterprises?"

The search engine returned a blank company splash page. No contact information. Nothing.

So far as he could tell, they had hired the smaller companies and stayed in the background. He could not find any single piece of information on who was behind Coniferous Enterprises. The challenge was to find out who the real culprits were.

Donovan stared at the screen momentarily. He'd reached a critical phase. Games were kids' stuff. Who got hurt if something went wrong? No one. And most gaming people understood and didn't sweat it too much. He even suspected they allowed hackers in to bleed the information to keep the public interested. But he was beginning to suspect that his father had been kidnapped, though he did not know when or by whom. And if they would do that, Donovan thought, what else had they done already?

It didn't take long for the last thought to sink in. His mind raced quickly through search possibilities, words, places, phrases and anything that could possibly turn up a lead. Tabs were open all over the phone. The network spun, trying to accommodate Donovan's fast mind.

"Come on, come on!" he barked at the spinning wheel on the screen.

"I found it!" Riley said from the back of the trailer.

"Found what?" Donovan placed the phone on top of the desk.

"A bunch of Dad's gear. All of it I think. Only it's scattered. I don't know if it was done on purpose," Riley said. "I think we should pick it up. Maybe there's a clue."

Donovan held the phone again and glowered at the frozen network.

"If only I had a better connection," he said.

"Beachball?" Riley asked.

"Big time! Don't worry, hopefully it will uncoil by the time we get back," Donovan said and followed Riley out of the trailer.

The four-wheeler roared around the forest. Under normal circumstances, two boys flying solo through the woods without adult supervision would have been heaven. As it was, Donovan and Riley barely uttered a word to one another. Riley idled back the machine as they started to navigate the thick underbrush. Both boys swatted at low branches that whipped and crawled at their faces. Spitting and sputtering, both boys looked at one another before Riley finally killed the motor.

"This is why I needed you. I couldn't get any further. We'll have to carry the equipment out to here," Riley said.

"Y'know, just because I was sitting down doesn't mean I wasn't working," Donovan defended.

"I didn't say you weren't. Take it easy. I understand. Hey,

if you brought the phone you might get reception out here," Riley chuckled.

"Right. Pine trees. Best cell phone signal conductivity ever devised," Donovan said and gestured to the shroud of trees. "I left it at the trailer."

"Come on. We've gotta get it!" Riley exclaimed.

"So tell me more about your tree walking," Kim snickered at Tanner.

"Forget it."

"I'm just teasing. Look, in all seriousness, the elders used to talk about a portage that happened long ago. Before white people. Y'know, ancient history. Anyway, this river was a very important part of our Mi'kmaq lifeblood. We would send our traders up to the head-waters with our best catch. If the catch was good, you gave respect to the land and Glooscap would help the traders find the path to the south river. He would part trees and make sure that those shallow waters were always full enough to allow even the heaviest canoe a safe passage. The traders would go to the southern shore, to the great ocean to trade with the southern people for whale oil. But the important thing was to show Glooscap respect."

"Do you think Glooscap has closed the path?" Tanner responded.

"To anyone not accustomed to these woods, when the sun descends, it can seem like the woods will grow around you."

Tanner looked around and shuddered. "So tell me more about Glooscap."

"If you're a good boy, you might be able to ask him yourself," Kim teased.

"Very funny," Tanner tried to chuckle.

"The elders say he has a wigwam in the woods. Hard to find. You have to ask to be able to use his canoe. His canoe can do many things. He's also a friend to all the wild animals in the forest. But you have to be careful. Glooscap is at odds with his brother Malsum. Malsum is full of mischief. He can make the animals do as he asks, too."

"Okay, I get it. So what do I have to do to ask Glooscap for some help?"

Kim was a little puzzled at his new friend who wasn't skeptical, dismissive or disrespectful. "Do you believe in these stories?" Kim cut to the chase.

"That there's much I don't know, and science can't explain everything?" Tanner paused. "With all my heart."

"That's not the same as believing in the spirits of the land," Kim countered.

Tanner shrugged. "We all have to believe what our senses tell us."

Kim studied him for a moment. Tanner turned and the two of them looked at one another for what seemed like an eternity. Tanner, completely relaxed, arms resting at his sides, lost his focus in Kim's face. Kim, a simmer of anger in his breath and a bout of disrespect in his smile, tried at first to stare down his new 'friend'. Humble him in some way. Why, and for what reason, he wasn't sure. They stood, locked eyes momentarily until Kim's emotion faded away. His mood altered. Hostility evaporated. Kim stuttered his breath at first before he caught a deep wind and inhaled deeply. One. Two. Three more deep breaths. The boys said nothing until a slow, singular motion pulled their eyes skyward.

An eagle, alone in the sky, circled above their heads.

Kim and Tanner stared in disbelief until the magnificent creature slowly descended towards them, circling downward. Just as it was about to touch earth, its wings pulled up and arrested its speed. With grace and power, it found a low branch with its talons. Folding in its wings, the eagle turned to face the two boys.

"Uh, did we do that?" Kim blurted.

"You have the spirit of Glooscap," the eagle said aloud.

Both boys swallowed hard.

"My father," Tanner stammered, "is in trouble. We think. We don't know where he is."

"Perhaps I can help," the eagle said and spread its wings.

"You are too kind. We would be grateful," Kim said and bowed to one knee.

"Rise. That is not necessary. I am not a god," the eagle continued.

Kim bounced up, a little embarrassed.

"I will help how I can," the eagle said and sprang from the branch. In no time, he had soared back into the heavens.

Kim looked at Tanner and gulped in disbelief.

"That was SO COOL!" Tanner exclaimed. "C'mon, let's go tell the guys!"

Tanner turned to burst through the woods before he felt a hand pull back on his shoulder.

"Don't!" Kim blurted.

Tanner turned, his face perplexed.

"Don't what?"

"Tell your friends."

"Why not?"

"Do I have to spell it out for you? You're with a native kid in the woods that you just met. Are you really going to tell them an eagle came down from the heavens to communicate telepathically? They'll think I made you try eating some strange mushrooms!"

"My friends are cool. They wouldn't say that!"

Kim searched for sincerity in his statement.

"Fine," he conceded, "but do you remember how to find your way back?"

"Even I can follow a bunch of broken branches, remember," Tanner said and peeled off into the woods.

Kim folded his arms and mulled over his options. Should he stay so the eagle could find him again? A little lost, a little bewildered, he shrugged before running off after his friend.

10

Alone in the Elements

The force of the powerful summer sun had long begun to fade on the western horizon. Great arcs of bright and rich red hues scuttled above the trees, climbing over themselves to reach into the horizon. A deep blue band hung just above the tree tops before giving way to a rich envelope of black emptiness. Ever so slowly, the distant stars woke, poking holes into the dark blanket to announce that they had just arisen.

As the watchful cosmos peered down, Tanner stood rooted in place. The small clearing seemed familiar but somehow the trees towered over him and shuffled ever closer, circling him. He began to back out of the clearing, certain the trees were moving to arrest his progress. The boughs blotted out the light from the stars. Kim reached his friend just as he started to retreat back into the forest.

"I sure wish we could find Glooscap's wigwam now!" Tanner exclaimed.

"We can't do that every time we need help. We'll survive. We just need to find a little shelter. It will get cold quick, but if we hurry and add some layers we should be alright. I'll get some tree branches, you go find some leaves," Kim said and started scrounging.

Tanner moved slowly through the forest. Some leaves had begun to change and fall. He gathered up as much as he could before turning his attention to the trees still flush with foliage. He grabbed the branch and shook.

A great tumble of leaves spilled out onto the forest floor. Leaping up from the pile, angry and perturbed, a squirrel screeched at Tanner.

"Sorry, sorry," Tanner replied. "My friend and I are out here alone. It's going to get cold tonight and we don't have warm shelter or clothing. We're not prepared."

The squirrel turned its head a moment before darting away.

"Guess it doesn't work every time," Tanner muttered and gathered his leaves. When he found a suitable tree, boughs low and heavy, he ducked underneath to start to make a bed for his camp. His jaw dropped and the leaves fluttered to the ground. Expecting to find a bed of sharp pine needles and raw dirt, Tanner instead bent down to a soft underlay of animal fur, dry straw and feathers, large enough for two boys!

He took off his shoes, rooted amongst the bedding and settled in comfortably. He almost fell immediately asleep when a sudden jolt reminded him Kim was still unaccounted for! Tanner sat up and rubbed his eyes. He was sure he'd only just rested a moment, but somehow he already felt rested. The gravity of their situation came back into sharp focus and he called out immediately: "KIM!"

There was no response. Tanner waited for a moment. He had somehow thought (with the recent turn of events) that he could close all his senses and reach out with just his mind to locate his friend. He took in a deep breath and scrunched up his face. He sensed...nothing.

Tanner grabbed his shoes and backed out of his shelter, mindful not to disturb the carefully crafted cocoon.

"I'm right here," Kim announced as he saw his friend back out from under the tree. Tanner jumped out of his footwear and fell to the ground. Kim placed his boughs around a neighbouring tree.

"Now, did you get any—" Kim noticed his friend had somehow lost his shoes. "I didn't scare you that badly, did I? Cripes, did you take your shoes off?"

Tanner got silently to his feet and plucked the boughs from Kim's hands.

"Okay, let's not get into a pissing contest over who can pick the best tree. Why did you pick that one?" Kim went on. Tanner nodded along with him as he neatly wove the plucked boughs seamlessly into the canopy of the nest. When he was finished, Tanner silently held open a branch and invited his friend inside.

Kim crouched and shuffled toward the opening. Tanner halted him.

"Shoes off please."

"But it's freezing!"

"Trust me."

Kim didn't know what to make of the situation. "Oh come o—" and the sight of the bedding greeted him. Fluffy, inviting and warm.

"This should get us through the night." Tanner shrugged. Shoes off, he crossed his legs.

"Uh, um, thanks," Kim stammered, sat down and immediately discarded his shoes. It wasn't long before the boys hunkered into their nest and were fast asleep.

"This really scares me. They should be back by now," Riley said.

"Yeah, well it's as dark as Hades out there. We don't have anything or anyway to look for them," Donovan reasoned.

"It's getting dark fast. Should we get our gear from the boats at the river?"

Riley considered the statement for a moment. He rifled through some of the bins in the office. As he popped the lid, a mixture or clothes, blankets and other assorted stuff sprang from the container.

"I think we'll be warmer here even if we don't find a sleeping bag. We'll be off the ground and away from the dew. And we don't have to try and put a tent up in the dark. If we can get enough to cover ourselves up, we should be alright," he said.

The gear, uncovered, was rough-hewn, grimy and worn. Donovan was hardly enticed.

"Hey, if you don't think it's a good idea, I'll understand. No skin off my back," Riley said, trying not to be offended.

"I think I'd rather find my own gear," Donovan said aloud.

"Be my guest. Here's the flashlight."

Donovan snatched the flashlight out of his friend's hand and marched to the back of the trailer. The doors swung wide. The beam tried to pierce out into the night but was greeted by a thick fog. The light reflected sharply back at Donovan.

"Aaacckkk," he said and put his hands up to protect his face. The flashlight clanked off the floor. He rubbed at his eyes as though he'd been stung.

Riley was startled by the way the fog repelled the light. He fought through the brightness which somehow reached deep into the trailer. He covered his eyes and swung blindly out to grab the handles of the doors. With wild stabs of his hands, he flailed at the night, feeling a thickness in the air, a presence more than fog.

"Shut the light off, Donovan!" he exclaimed. Donovan, momentarily blinded, couldn't reach the flashlight. It continued to burn into the fog. The fog slowly crept inside.

"I can't see it!" Donovan exclaimed.

Riley continued to swing until he finally found the latch. He jerked at it. The door didn't budge. He tugged again and almost lost his grip. He lost his balance and almost fell out of the trailer. He could feel his hands slipping when he reached out with his other hand and hauled the door shut. As the door swung closed, the fog was cut off. The light dimmed until a small circle glowed on the door.

Donovan waved at the air. In the faint light, a few molecules of fog lingered. He was about to look away when he noticed the specks floating away from the trailer as if being pulled back out into the night.

"Tell me you didn't just see that?" Riley exclaimed.

"I know what I saw, but I can't explain it," Donovan conceded.

A long moment passed between them.

Donovan looked at Riley. Riley tensed as he prepared for Donovan to discuss what they just experienced.

"Are we going to sleep on the floor?" Donovan finally asked.

Riley leaned back against the wall of the trailer. To his left, he saw a rope stretch its way up to the ceiling. He noticed what appeared to be a piece of plywood hanging against the wall. He reached up and tugged at the edge. It held tight. Riley followed the rope where a clever knot held it firm. He tugged. With a whirr and a groan, the plywood flopped down, parallel to the floor.

"It doesn't look like we'll have to," Riley beamed.

Donovan looked around, found a similarly inconspicuous rope and gave it a hearty yank. Another cot lowered itself into position. In short order both boys rummaged for some warmer layers and prepared for bed.

"I really wish there was more we could do for Tanner and Kim!" Donovan exclaimed.

"We'll do better by them if we both don't go out and get lost. They'll be alright," Riley responded before adding silently, *I hope!*

11

Rallying Cry

For all four boys, it was a very restless sleep. The journey, the hazards, the new friendship and the mystery of the disappearance all played itself out in their minds. The adrenaline and excitement made it difficult to unwind.

Tanner, in particular, straddled the deep edge of wakefulness. It was as though he'd left himself standing outside by the tree.

He would recall how, the next day, the animals returned to him, one by one, to share themselves with him. The squirrels and chipmunks showed the journey of gathering feathers and fur for their nest. Word of the boys' plight had spread to every animal in the forest. Every animal, in some way, shared a piece of themselves to save Tanner and Kim.

Through it all, the eagle sat on his perch, nodding at each creature who assisted. Fox, rabbits, squirrels, raccoons and chipmunks had all participated in the effort. When the last animal sat, the eagle swooped down and seized Tanner in his talons. The great bird powered them both into flight. Rising up farther into the sky, it wasn't long before they were both coasting on the great winds. He could sense the cool air in the atmosphere but was never cold. It seemed they had flown forever. A great expanse of trees and forest spread out infinitely beneath them. Like the eagle, he could quickly catch motion and let it arrest his attention. His eyes darted beneath him. Where there was activity, there was life.

A headlight switched on in the darkness. Then more. It wasn't long until the vast patch of an empty field sprang from the forest. The eagle started to slow. He banked into a circle and slowly began his descent. Trucks, buildings, activity. Even in the dark of night, the oasis in the forest was buzzing with activity. A small, portable building, not much bigger than the trailer Roy used, echoed light from every window except two dark panes at the back. Occasionally the light was broken by a figure passing in front of the window. Outside, burly men stood guard beside the door. The men shuffled away from the opening as a stout, silver-haired man burst past them.

A noise thundered in the trailer.

Tanner was perplexed. The picture was vivid. Clear. He could see the scope of what he needed to do and the challenge of fulfilling his goal.

The eagle carried on. The next thing Tanner remembered, he stood outside the boughs of his nest. Every animal, every spirit suddenly surrounded him. Tanner nodded at them, touching them all.

Suddenly the darkness engulfed them like a shroud and Tanner stood alone again, locked in the eagle's gaze.

"You have uncovered that which is great, powerful and beyond all knowing. Use what you know wisely, with respect, and this spirit will serve you well." The eagle continued to lock eyes with him. The eagle finally broke his gaze and flew off into the night. Tanner tumbled back into a deep sleep.

"Tell me how. Help me understand."

The voice tried to be reasonable.

"I wish I could, sir. I wish I could. Our drillers have never seen anything like this before," someone answered back.

"I'm sure of that. Why else do you think I'm here? If these loogans don't figure this out, I'll go down there and run the drill myself," the voice thundered.

"Sir, the geologists say the shale is brittle and the diamond bit should have no trouble at all."

"So what is it!?" the White Wizard thundered.

The men looked at one another and swallowed hard.

"Every time we pull the drill out of the ground, we expect to find shale, right?"

"And it isn't!?"

"No. It's nothing that should be expected at that depth."

"What!? What is it then!?"

"It's organic material."

"And you're absolutely, one hundred percent positive about that?"

"It's certainly no rock I've ever seen," the driller responded.

The White Wizard sat back in his chair. The driller across the desk instinctively took a step back. The temper and fury of the man was legendary. He burned with intensity. His brows furrowed into a sharp, piercing gaze. It was like a spell. He could root his quarry to the ground with a simple look. The terror pierced even the heartiest of men with paralysis. Even the flower on his desk recoiled in fear.

"Have you tested it to see what kind of organic material?"

"The lab is looking at it right now."

"But you mean to tell me that with every hole we've dug, this exact same thing is happening?" the White Wizard demanded.

"Without fail. Drilling has halted at different depths, but certainly not as deep as we need to fracture properly. It's almost as if the earth is rejecting us," the driller responded.

"Frack one anyway," the White Wizard commanded.

"Excuse me, sir?"

"You heard me. We're bleeding money every second! We're wasting our time here. We need results. The next well you drill, however deep it goes, I want you to fracture it anyway," the White Wizard said.

"Fracture it anyway?" the driller questioned.

"You heard me. I don't want questions, I want results. We'll punch our ticket into the rock whether it wants us to or not!"

"But—sir," the driller stammered.

"But NOTHING. I run this ship and THIS IS HOW we're going to do it. If something doesn't work and you keep trying, that's the definition of insanity. Or, in your case, stupidity," the White Wizard thundered.

The driller held his breath. The White Wizard glowered over the table at him. Without moving or saying anything, the stocky man seemed to grow and take over the entire room. The burly guards outside the door quivered in their boots. They looked over at one another to see if the other noticed the shiver of frosty air.

"It's dangerous. We barely contained the last anomaly." The driller's voice was barely above a whisper.

"I don't care if this village burns to the ground. We will get what we came for! Do you understand?"

The intensity of the gaze of the White Wizard burned at the eyes of the man seated across from him. Internally the choice rested within the driller to get out of the chair, walk out the door and never return. Yet the man felt captured in a strange grip that he couldn't explain. A grip that wouldn't allow him the right to command his legs to move or his mind to function. In the company of the White Wizard, his free will was detained. He was somehow made aware of his thoughts but couldn't act on them. He bowed his head in servitude, mumbled something under his breath and ever so slowly shuffled out the door.

When Tanner arose, it was daybreak. If they could have seen it through the forest thickets, the boys would have noticed a blue hue on the horizon. It was going to be another clear day. Tanner rolled over, still groggy, still a little disbelieving.

"Did the eagle visit last night?" Kim asked.

Tanner nodded silently, "yes, I know where my Dad is."

Kim was relieved.

It was difficult for either boy to find the words to express the spectrum of thoughts and emotions that the night had stirred. They slowly pulled on their shoes. Some time passed before Kim broke the silence.

"I don't know about you, but I'm hungry and more than a little sore. I'm sure you are too. It's not too far to the camp. Let's regroup with Riley and Donovan, quickly get some food and go get your dad." The boys gathered themselves together and bowed their heads in gratitude. Though the animals had returned to the forest, their presence lingered.

The rear of the trailer creaked and heaved. Riley bolted upright and reached for the flashlight. He looked to Donovan who was just waking up. He rubbed his eyes as the trailer continued to shuffle. The back door yawned open, letting the early morning sun stretch into the trailer. Both boys grimaced as the intense light reached their eyes. Tanner and Kim stood grinning at the door.

"Oh thank gawd!" Riley exclaimed and leapt from the cot. The other boys flung around some pre-packaged cereal bars and stomped around the trailer.

"What did you find?" Tanner asked.

"Dad's gear all over hell's half acre," Riley responded.

"Good, I think we're going to need it."

"Need it?" Donovan asked.

"That sounds to me like you know something," Riley commented.

"We didn't find them, but we know where they are," Tanner said.

"Then let's go get them."

"It isn't quite that simple," Kim retorted.

"We're sure they're okay. So far. If we don't do something, I don't know how long that will last," Tanner explained.

Riley swallowed hard.

"That might explain the news clippings," Donovan conceded. "If I could ever get the network..."

"You can try, but I think we need to do something," Tanner stated.

"Uh, like what?"

"Like a distraction of some kind. A big one."

Donovan gulped hard. Riley shifted on his feet. Kim crossed his arms over his chest.

"And what do you have in mind?" Riley asked.

"I saw what I think is a tailings pond," Tanner said.

"No. No. No. No. No. Wrong. Bad Idea. I know what you're thinking. Tanner, this isn't some prank you do at Halloween,"

Donovan said.

"Hear me out. We divert some of the tailings into the river," Tanner started over Donovan's objections, "and start a fire."

"That's madness!" Donovan bellowed.

"No, wait," Riley said, "it makes sense. It's thicker than water. It will float on top until it burns itself out."

"Then the water snuffs out the fire," Kim said.

Suddenly the idea didn't seem too ludicrous after all.

"I can't believe you're even considering this. We could set the whole forest on fire. That's arson!" Donovan protested.

"You know what, guys? Do you know what I talked about with my dad before he decided to do this? He said that no matter what happens to him, he can look back and say he had almost no regrets about the choices he's made. He said he wanted me to know that I don't need to wait to learn that lesson. That lesson starts today. Right now. So, I've made up my mind. Because I'd hate to look back on this moment and say, "what if I'd only...?" So wait for help. Wait for whatever you want. I'm going to do what I can to help my Dad!" Tanner stormed out of the trailer.

An uncomfortable silence hung in the air. The boys were at a stalemate. They needed consensus to proceed. Riley turned away and noticed one of the newspaper clippings on the floor. He picked up the paper and read the headline aloud:

"Three Workers Dead in Industrial Accident. Coniferous Holdings..." Riley read aloud.

"Coniferous," Donovan echoed. He pushed his way past the other two boys to reach for the smartphone. The screen sprang to life. The network was functioning.

"Found not liable," he scrolled further, "investigation leads to dropped charges. Not criminally responsible. It's a pattern.

They change names, they change countries but still manage to operate." He wiped sweat from his brow. "They get away with it. Every time. And they always find a way to maintain stock performance." The screen froze. The connection went cold.

Donovan looked to Riley and Kim and nodded. Riley walked out of the trailer and hauled Tanner back inside.

Tanner, still trying to plead his case, looked at the clues on the bench. He picked up the newspaper clipping and blurted out loud, "That's HIM! That's the guy in my dream."

Riley grabbed the paper and shared it with Donovan, "John Gerryston, aka the White Wizard?"

"He's bad news. He gets away with everything!"

Tanner took a deep breath and pitched the article away.

"I can make you a distraction!" Riley said with conviction.

Tanner looked at Kim, "And we can get them out. We have... a way."

Donovan took a deep breath before nodding his head. "Wait, I found another walkie," he said. "You are not going out there without some form of communication. It might be antique, but it works!"

He tossed the second walkie-talkie toward Tanner and Kim. Tanner tucked it onto his belt.

"Check. Check!" Donovan said into the device.

"Uh, 10-4, copy," Tanner responded.

"Copy. Just say copy," Riley interjected. Tanner grinned and pulled Kim with him out of the trailer.

"I really think, with your dad's equipment, we should be able to create a different kind of distraction," Donovan pleaded. "He has so many effects, we should be able to do anything we want. Why don't we do a fog blanket? It tripped us up, didn't it? It's not dangerous. It certainly won't cause a forest fire."

"But it won't lead the bad guys away. And it won't catch anyone else's attention, either. We need to catch these guys in the act. The best way to do that is to take the fight to them with the element of surprise," Riley responded.

"Oh, it'll be a surprise alright. It'll be a surprise if we don't burn the whole forest down," Donovan said.

"I can make this work," Riley ignored him.

The ATV zoomed around the forest floor, equipment heaped in the small trailer they hauled along behind them. Hoses, clamps, the valve tree. Riley had everything in mind as he mentally assembled the gear. He was beginning to appreciate the joy his father had in creating an effect. Being responsible for a certain element and pulling it all together, and in the end, seeing your work displayed on a large screen for many others to see. Though he wasn't working alongside his stepfather, he felt the connection to the older man tighten.

The ATV reached the edge of the tailings pond and pulled to a stop. Donovan reached over the side of the trailer and tugged off a bundle of hose. He untied the knot that held it together and rolled it toward the river. Riley rolled another hose up the hill toward the tailings pond.

"Don't we need a pump of some kind?" Donovan asked.

"I hope not. I'm hoping that we can draw the liquid out with gravity," Riley responded.

"Right, gravity. Unfortunately, it appears we'll have to stick the end of the hose down into the pond. Looks like we'll have to suck on the hose to create an air displacement," Donovan answered.

"Air displacement?" Riley asked.

"A vacuum. If there is no source of air to displace the liquid, then it can't move. Unless it's introduced. That's how people siphon gas out of a tank." Donovan answered.

"Hmm, makes sense," Riley agreed.

"It does. In the lab. But you're always telling me theory and reality don't always agree," Donovan conceded.

"How's it coming along, guys?" came the voice from the walkie.

"We're just about ready. Are you at the site?" Donovan responded.

"Yeah, we're here," Tanner responded. He looked over his shoulder at Kim. As the two crouched, Tanner noticed a branch dangling toward the ground. They were closer to the location last night than he realized.

"We just need to stick the last hose together. We'll be ready in no time. Do you want us to ignite it or should we wait for you?"

12

Inside the Compound

Tanner took a deep breath. The fate of the entire forest rested with this decision. If he let fear take hold and prevent him from doing anything, there was no telling what might happen. But knowing the risks and taking action might still cause great harm. There was no good answer.

"The only thing I know for sure," he remembered his father tell him, *"is to look back with minimal regrets. And I regret more the things I DIDN'T do."*

He tilted his head back and looked up. He knew he wasn't an expert, and he was quite sure he'd never forget the eagle that had whisked him away in his dream, but wasn't that a turkey vulture circling overhead? A moment of doubt crept into his mind. Tanner was about to look away when Kim pointed to the air.

The turkey vulture had company. More birds joined the procession in the air: crows, ravens, hawks. Above them still, the eagle rode the heavens, the lord of the sky. His confidence returned, Tanner sighed again and looked at the chain link fence imposed in front of him.

"First obstacle," Kim pointed out.

The top of the tall fence was adorned with six rows of barbed wire, taut and imposing. Beyond the obstacle, a small collection of working trailers gathered in random formation. From their position, the two boys couldn't discern any human activity. It appeared as though the site was already abandoned.

"I've cleared these before. At least it's not razor wire," Kim said.

Tanner stayed his hand. "I have a feeling we won't have to touch it."

Kim wasn't sure what his friend meant until a slight movement caught his attention. A porcupine, waddling in its own peculiar way, ambled past them toward the fence. The creature stopped when he reached the obstruction. He glanced around, quietly sniffing the air before his feet went to work. The front claws took on a feverish, frenzied action. Tanner and Kim stared in disbelief as the small mammal disappeared in no time. Though they understood they seemed to have all the woodland creatures assisting their efforts, the extent of that help continued to surprise them.

Just a few feet inside of the fence, the boys looked on as the soil bubbled and moved. The dirt caved in as the porcupine popped up out of the ground just inside the fence. Tanner didn't hesitate.

"Ignite," he said calmly into the walkie-talkie.

"Whatever you do, do not light the end of the hose. The fire could ignite so fast it spreads up the hose," Donovan warned.

"Okay. Get the blowtorch. When the valve shuts off, ignite the river," Riley said.

"Me?" Donovan squeaked.

"Take a rag. A stick. Anything that will carry a flame when you throw it. That way you can start the fire a safe distance away," Riley responded.

Donovan hurried off. He burst into the trailer, eyes darting across shelves and material.

'What would ignite and stay lit as I toss it into the water?' he mumbled to himself.

He tossed a couple of things into the middle of the trailer before he settled on a few items: an old rag, oily and well-used, and a plastic bottle. Satisfied with his selection, he darted back out of the trailer.

It was the smell that met him first. Unmistakable. Acrid. The lingering stench after a car pulled out of a garage. Donovan stopped in his tracks and went back inside. It was all well and good if the river went up in a blaze, but what about them? He spotted a fire extinguisher and added it to his items.

Donovan was scrambling down the hill when the rumbling ATV came into focus. Riley pulled the machine to a stop. Donovan heaved his things onto the trailer and climbed on behind.

"I couldn't wait for you. You were taking too long," Riley exclaimed.

"You shut the valve off? Please tell me you shut the valve off!" Donovan pleaded.

"Of course, I even pulled the hose back out of the water," Riley exclaimed.

"Okay, great. Let's get this show on the road!" Donovan responded and the ATV sped off through the woods.

It wasn't until the White Wizard himself burst out of the

trailer that Tanner crawled under the fence. Both boys sprang up on the other side like a pair of gophers. Their heads darted around, scanning for trouble. As the White Wizard disappeared from view, they both sprang up and cleared the open ground between the fence and trailer in record time.

"Okay," Kim muttered as both boys slammed their backs against the side of the trailer. "Now what?"

From their vantage point, both boys could see the faint lick of smoke crest the top of the forest trees. The wisp was soon joined by a crescendo of dark, dense smoke. In no time, the plume was noticed and the entire site whipped into a frenzy of activity. Fire alarms went off. Emergency sirens soon followed. The few remaining workers scrambled about.

Given the harried response to the fire, the boys could have walked right through the front door. Instead, Tanner flipped down to his back and rolled underneath the portable trailer. Kim followed.

Both boys crawled deeper under the trailer. Tanner stopped as he noticed small particles of wood dust. The gently falling particles turned bigger and larger in the early morning sun. Instead of drifting aimlessly to the ground, the heavy particles were tumbling in earnest. Great heaves of sawdust cascaded to the soil.

Tanner crawled as close to the fissure in the flooring as he could. He closed his eyes, reached up and his hand magically appeared in the room above. The plywood disintegrated away.

As the hands reached up into the room, Warren, Marshal and Roy scurried away to a corner. They weren't bound or tied, but fatigue slowed their nerves.

"What the—!?" Marshal started to yell before Warren clamped a hand over his mouth.

"Dad?" Tanner whispered.

"Tanner!?" Warren responded before flopping down on the floor.

"Can you squeeze through?" Tanner asked.

"I don't see how," Warren said as he eyed the small break in the floor where Tanner's arms squeezed into the room.

"The floor is weak. It will give. Be fast. Trust me. Grab my hand and I'll pull you through."

Warren didn't hesitate. In no time he was somersaulting under the trailer.

"How the hell did he do—" Marshal couldn't finish his sentence before he too was pulled through the opening. Roy didn't hesitate. He dove after them.

When the dads regained their bearings, Tanner was already at the edge of the trailer. He looked up and saw the procession of crows, ravens and eagles had all followed away from the compound.

"We've got to keep this under control!" they heard through the floorboards. Warren crawled back a little until he could hear the discussion in the room above.

"It was bad enough when we couldn't drill through the soil. It's happened before. Not that unusual. I get that. Now a hoard of wild birds are fanning an inferno on the water! You can be the one to tell that to the White Wizard!"

Warren's jaw dropped before he crawled back to the rest.

"Tell me what!?!" thundered the voice as it stormed up the stairs into the trailer.

"We, uh, should get out of here," Warren suggested.

"Right, I second that," Marshal agreed.

The faint noise of emergency sirens could be heard in the distance.

"I don't want to catch the blame for this mess," Roy confessed and started to crawl out from under the trailer. The others started to follow.

"How could they blame you?" Tanner asked.

"They claimed the drilling problems were being caused by eco-terrorists," Warren explained.

"Wait, I've got an idea," Tanner said as he pulled the walkie-talkie off of the clip on his belt. "What's the police frequency?" Roy stopped and crawled back under the trailer.

"I know," Roy said. Tanner handed him the walkie-talkie. Roy pushed the channel and frequency buttons and quickly tuned to the emergency channel.

"How did you know how to do that?" Warren started to ask.

"It comes in handy on occasion," Roy explained. He took the walkie to the weak point in the floor he'd just crawled out of. He reached up, pushed on the floor and jammed the walkie in by the antenna.

"Now, let's just make sure the 'talk' button stays on and we're good to go."

Roy turned around after making sure the antenna was safely secured and felt a hand grab his wrist.

"Go!" he yelled to his friends.

Marshal and Warren turned to look back at their friend as he fought desperately to break free. He managed to wriggle loose and scrambled to catch up. The others rolled quickly out from underneath the trailer. As they struggled to their feet, they failed to notice the long shadow looming over them.

"Yeah, that's exactly what you can go ahead and tell the press. Eco-terrorists or activists or whatever you want to call them were apprehended on site. They committed a terrorist act and were arrested by security staff. Official authorities are being notified. There were some injuries. Some may be life-threatening. The site is still too dangerous for police and fire crews. No one knows the extent of their activities. I repeat, site is still too dangerous for police and fire. We are on lockdown!" The White Wizard hung up the phone. He turned to face the two boys and three dads.

"Now, as for our terrorists..." the White Wizard said and chuckled menacingly. "That WAS a clever little plan you had. I wasn't going to go so far as to start an inferno, mind you."

"Then what were you going to do?" Tanner blurted.

"Tanner. Stop!" Warren exclaimed and winked at his son.

"We caught these trespassers and were about to issue an appropriate release to the authorities," the White Wizard explained.

"Trespassers!" Roy repeated incredulously.

"You were on leased company property," came the voice of Harry Eaglesmith. The door to the trailer opened. An older Mi'kmaq man stepped into the room. Tanner recoiled as he looked. The man's eyes were closed, the lids unmoving. Light licks of red pigment, embedded in his skin, stretched into a faded feather at the right side of his face. His skin was blotched and sullen. He carried the weighted fortunes of his people on his sloped, weary shoulders.

"This site would have provided for my people. Jobs. Opportunity. Prosperity. Respect. Instead, the drills, somehow, did not operate," Harry said and squinted. He looked in the direction of Tanner and Kim.

"The seismic tests told us there was abundant gas deposits. And yet our drills could only get so deep into the soil," the

112

White Wizard said. "Our company invested significant capital. This was an expensive undertaking. We are not in the business of NOT seeing a return."

"So when you came along, we knew we could package you as eco-terrorists. If the place burns to the ground and leaves no evidence," Harry explained, "that's an opportunity we can't afford to let slip."

"What's our move now?" Riley asked.

"No matter what way you slice it, we set fire to the river. It was a controlled fire, but a huge danger nonetheless," Donovan observed.

"No, I mean *now*. What's our move now? Do we wait here or do we clear out? Should we go find them?" Riley said.

The walkie crackled to life. Donovan and Riley both listened intently. They were now part of the conversation in the trailer.

"The soil would not let us drill down...and then you came along..."

"How are they getting him to confess like that?" Riley wondered.

"Who cares, it won't make a bit of difference unless someone hears it," Donovan whipped the smartphone out of his pocket. He dialled 911 and pressed the walkie to the speaker.

"Is this the best we can do?" Riley wondered. The boys sat nestled against a tree stump. From their vantage point, they could make out the ordered chaos inside the compound.

"What if someone finds the hose from the tailings pond that goes into the river? They'll get blamed for this mess no matter how strong the confession," Riley exclaimed.

"But the fire will go out. As soon as the chemicals burn off, the water will snuff out the rest," Donovan said. "In fact, it should finish shortly."

"I can feel heat. Even from here," Riley confessed.

Donovan turned his head. He closed his eyes, trusting his senses. He took a deep breath. Like a faint mist, he could feel the heat through the simmering shadows of the summer morning. It felt like the shine of a campfire on his face.

"It shouldn't be that warm. We're far away. Suppose the trees caught fire?" Donovan said with uncertainty.

"We didn't put in that much. It was concentrated on the water. There's no way," Riley said and looked at Donovan intently.

"Unless..." Donovan scratched his chin.

"Unless what?" Riley asked.

"If you listened to that conversation, then we're playing right into their hands. This is exactly what they want," Donovan said.

"Somebody turned the valve back on! We need to shut off the valve," Riley exclaimed and bolted back into the forest. Donovan hesitated. They had no plan and no knowledge about what might lie ahead. Worse yet, if they got caught, they would be of no use to their friends. He had just turned to follow Riley when he saw his friend marching slowly toward him.

13

The Growing Inferno

"Uncle Harry, I don't understand. You don't even know what chemicals they use. What it might do to our drinking water?" Kim blurted.

Harry shrugged off the weight of the accusation. He paraded around the room. The White Wizard smirked from behind his desk. Two burly men came toward the five of them with a large roll of duct tape. Tanner took a quick survey of the room. They outnumbered their captors and could make a break. What was preventing them? Tanner looked around for a gun or anything of that nature. He saw nothing. He looked at Warren and gestured as though they should fight their way out.

As subtly as he could, Warren shook his head from side to side. Not a good idea. The burly men gripped their arms and pinned them behind their backs. A couple of wraps of tape later, they were shoved into the same room at the back.

"Our people are suffering, young one. Suffering from substance abuse. Poverty. Lack of opportunity," Harry confessed. "These resources are our chance to create wealth. It would ease our suffering and give us purpose. Restore our pride."

"By sacrificing your health? Our health? The health of the

river?" Tanner blurted, feeling all the eyes in the room spin his way. He wanted to hide.

The door burst open again. Two workers ploughed through the room with a sheet of plywood and tool belts. They marched to the room at the back of the trailer.

"However they managed to escape, make sure it doesn't happen again!" the White Wizard thundered. With each rumble of his voice, everyone in the room shrank a little. The workers looked around for the point of escape unsuccessfully.

"Hurry up!" the White Wizard barked again.

The two men shrugged and pasted the board over the window. The plywood was quickly screwed into place. Tanner had to suppress a laugh.

His hands and feet bound, Tanner was the last one forced into the room at the back. The White Wizard took one last glance around the space. Satisfied there was no means of escape, he spun on his heel and slammed the door behind him.

No sooner had he left, than the five prisoners started working feverishly to free themselves from the tape.

A gust of wind whipped up around the trailer. It was followed by several more until the entire structure started to rock violently. Anyone standing suddenly lost their balance and fell.

"What the hell is that?!" came the voices on the other side of the door. The violent rocking settled, allowing the captors to regain their feet. The White Wizard surged out the door. He recoiled in horror. Around them, surrounding the site, the sky pounded with the beat of flapping feathers.

The White Wizard charged back into the trailer. Still struggling to find his footing, Harry Eaglesmith was pulled to his feet. The breath of the White Wizard was right in his face.

"I'm going to say this so you will be sure to hear me. You better not let me down," the silver-haired White Wizard gripped Harry by the shoulder and pulled him out of the trailer.

Harry and the White Wizard scrambled out the door, men following after them until only Tanner and his party were left in the trailer. The door slammed shut behind them until only shrieks and screams could be heard in the distance.

"Judas!" Roy exclaimed. "Is it the Apocalypse?"

Tanner was easing through the split in the floor. The others scrambled to follow. This time when they tumbled to the earth below, a tunnel swallowed them up. Not stopping to question where they were or where they were going, the party started moving. They crawled on their hands and knees as fast as their limbs would carry them.

On in the darkness they crawled for what seemed like an eternity. Neither boy nor man opened their eyes to question or comment. It was a tight squeeze. Space was limited. No one wanted to acknowledge the darkness surrounding them.

Yet somehow the roof above was not quite as solid as the walls. Tanner reasoned that the tunnel was shallow. The give of the roof was letting them move along at a brisk pace. Despite being on their hands and knees, Tanner had a good idea they were already past the fence that surrounded the perimeter. Any minute now they should break onto the surface.

They popped up out of the ground right and startled Riley. Donovan was just catching up and the two boys looked stunned as their friends and fathers appeared seemingly out of nowhere. One by one, they reached in to pull them out of the tunnel.

The heat of the fire hit them as they sprang to their feet.

"It's out of control!" Riley exclaimed. Tanner thought quickly.

"It wasn't us. Someone must have turned the valve back on," Donovan said.

"We need to shut it down. It's going to start a forest fire!" Warren bellowed.

Had he taken the time to look Warren would have noticed the blackened sky overhead wasn't caused by smoke. Every winged creature in the Acadian realm hovered around the edge of the forest beating their wings. Tanner looked up and saw the glorious eagle tending the situation. He didn't know how long they'd been doing their part, but he knew it couldn't last indefinitely. They needed help, and the sooner the better.

"They're keeping the flames from the forest. We're running out of time. They can't keep this up! We have to do something," Tanner pleaded to his dad.

"What about the fans?" Roy asked, "and the rain towers? Did these miners confiscate my gear?

"No, we managed to find what we needed to start the fire," Riley confessed.

"YOU started the fire?" Roy asked. The dads looked at the boys.

"We needed a distraction. It was only a small amount of fluid. It was supposed to burn off and…"

"Too late to lay any blame now. We need a plan and we need it quick," Warren said.

"We think they put the hose back into the tailings pond and now they're draining it into the river," Donovan said.

"We need to cut off the source and put out the fire," Tanner said.

"Hoo boy, I wish I had my team. I can make a downpour but I'm going to need some help," Roy said.

Putting his arms around Donovan, Riley volunteered. Marshal was soon to follow.

"We've got the hose," Warren said and gripped his arms around the other two boys.

Warren, Tanner and Kim stumbled along the bluff above the river. So far they encountered no one during their travels. In fact, they were surprised to find the area abandoned.

"Looks like someone called to evacuate," Warren exclaimed.

"Then it shouldn't be too hard to turn off the valve," Kim said before a slight shutter of light caught his attention. Curious, he turned to look at what made the shimmer. Kim squinted and trained his eyes on the slight flicker of muscle. Long hairs streaked through the sun. It wasn't a snake. It was a tail!

Kim wanted to run and scream, but found himself paralyzed. The Great Cat crept out from behind a rotted tree stump.

"You are not the only one to command the beasts of this world, my brother Glooscap," came the familiar voice of the White Wizard.

Tanner and Warren turned back when they heard the voice. The cat, a tan-coloured giant, glowered at Kim. He crouched and crept toward his prey. Kim wanted to run, shout, scream but couldn't will his body to move. When the urge to leap away finally came to him, his movement was clumsy. His leg caught in a rock and he fell heavily.

As though hurled from the hands of a bowler, a black bear leapt from the bluff and swatted a mighty paw in the direction of the Great Cougar. The big cat struck out in defense and bounded away as the black bear thundered by with an ineffective strike. As suddenly as he had appeared, the White Wizard slid away in the confusion.

The bear spun to face the cougar again, a shimmer of light glistening off the fur of the animal. The charge had wounded both animals, but the bear had gotten the worst of the first exchange. Angry, the black bear rose up on his hind legs and roared at his adversary. The cat licked the blood from his front paws before crouching to strike again.

"Quickly, while they're distracted," Tanner urged and tugged at his father. Warren didn't budge. He knelt over Kim's prone body.

"He must have hit his head when he saw the cougar."

"We can't leave him. But we need to shut off the valve."

"Tanner, I need to stay here and protect Kim. You can shut off the valve," Warren said.

Tanner caught Warren looking at him. An easy grin tugged at Tanner's mouth. Right then, Warren knew, without a doubt, what had lain dormant in his son. It was the first true glance into the man he would become. Tanner took a wide berth around the combatants and ploughed into the forest. The cougar saw his movement and lunged after Tanner. Tanner leapt away with all his strength. He hit the ground and rolled. The cougar missed.

Tanner struggled to regain his footing. His foot was wedged under a rock. He pulled and tugged to no avail. He searched around for something, anything, he could use to defend himself. As he did, the hot breath of the cougar hit him in the face. He was perched on the same rock that held Tanner's foot. A low rumble escaped the cat's throat. The kind of deep rumble that could paralyze helpless prey. Behind him, the tail waved back and forth menacingly. The animal was taking his time. The cougar licked his lips before reaching a front paw high into the air.

Tanner flinched in the shadow of the fatal blow. He curled his hands up to his face to protect himself. He clenched his jaw, ready to scream. But then...nothing.

Somehow his foot came loose and Tanner slid out from under the rock. He scurried away as fast as he could. He saw a short stick on the forest floor and he clutched the stick in front of his chest, ready to swing.

He clenched his jaw, feeling each heaving breath pass through his teeth. Through squinted eyes, he saw the black bear rear back on his legs, mouth wide. Below him, the cougar lay prone and helpless. Down the bear pounced. Tanner turned away. The roaring stopped.

When he could open his eyes again, the Great Cat lay motionless. The bear walked past his fallen enemy, trailing blood with each slow paw print. The animal slipped away where he would allow himself to accept the fate that awaited him.

Tanner scrambled down the bluff. The blaze, intense but contained, greeted his descent. He looked up in the sky as the eagle soared overhead. Below him, scores of lesser birds flapped to contain the fire. Tanner, relieved that the blaze was contained, breathed a short sigh of relief. He turned away from the river only to feel the heat intensify. The birds, once in unison, had begun to tire. In that fatigue, some of the lesser great birds broke formation. Ravens had appeared from the nether regions of the deep forest and attacked the heart of the effort.

Tanner turned his head. Standing on top of the bluff was the White Wizard and Harry Eaglesmith. Tanner took a deep breath and charged up the hill.

14

River Rescue

Roy tore through the trailer as quickly as he could with his son trailing after him. Roy searched frantically before he found an empty bin and dumped it into Riley's hands. It was followed by a stream of miscellaneous gadgets and tools. When the bin was full, Riley handed it off to Marshal and Donovan. They dumped it into the back of the four-wheeler. They both looked at each other, curious, scared and confused.

"Don't worry son," Marshal started, "be open and don't pretend to know everything. If you have any questions, just ask."

Roy stood for a moment, thinking hard. He looked at his crew. As he had done many times before, he took a quick assessment of their talents and abilities before deciding how best to deploy them. Explaining items to assemble was going to be a challenge. He could only make decisions on what he thought they knew. Marshal was only with them a short time and from what he could understand, the man wasn't the most adept with his hands. But he seemed willing to follow instructions.

"We need to work in teams if my plan is going to work. There's no time to explain every little item. Ask important questions only, save the juice on the walkies. Marshal, do you remember where we set up the rain towers?"

Marshal nodded.

"Do you think you and Donovan can move them as close to the fire as you possibly can?"

"Done," Marshal said. "Towers only or towers and hose?"

"Towers first, then hose. We should be ready by then."

Marshal tapped Donovan on the shoulder.

Riley interrupted for a moment as he held the radio to his mouth, "Donovan, Check. Check!"

Donovan pulled the walkie from his belt and responded, "That's a big 10-4!" He grinned back at his friend before he and Marshal ran into the forest. It wasn't long before they were swallowed by the thickets, their movements sheltered by small wafts of black smoke. Roy looked to the top of the trees to give him guidance.

"The heat and the smoke will rise. Don't let that scare you, son. It will appear worse up there," Roy said and pointed. "As long as that smoke doesn't get too thick near the ground, we're going to have a chance. If this doesn't work, we'll have to evacuate. And if it really doesn't work," Roy's voice trailed off, "then I won't have anywhere else to run." His thoughts drifted momentarily. Acadia was the last place he thought he'd get himself into trouble. It seemed so safe. So simple.

"I missed that last part, can you repeat it?" Riley asked.

Roy ignored his stepson, "The big fans are in Harry's shed. You and I will get them onto the trailer and move them as close to the fire as we can."

"I got it. What about a pump?" Riley asked.

"For the rain tower. Right," Roy's mind was starting to race. Riley could sense his stepfather didn't have complete control over his thoughts. Roy's face went blank.

"Dad, if it helps, I can start the fans and I can drive the four-wheeler," Riley offered. "That way you can assemble the pump."

"Great idea. Once the fans start, we only need to aim them. I can trust you to do that yourself. Idle them low until the water starts," Roy said.

Tanner marched along the forest ridge. Only now, several minutes removed from the life and death struggle with the large woodland predators, had his heart beat returned to normal. He let himself be guided by what he remembered seeing in his dream. If he let his mind get distracted thinking about all that had happened, he'd surely paralyze with fear.

As he walked, he felt the intensity of the heat flush his face. It was a good sign he was headed in the right direction. He slowed his pace, hoping to avoid detection as long as possible. *If anything*, he thought, *they might hear the pounding in my chest before they hear me coming.*

He was just catching his breath when he saw the faint shadows of two figures through small wafts of smoke. Tanner took a deep breath to steady his nerves. It didn't seem to have any effect. His heart jumped into his throat. He approached the adults cautiously.

"We need to shut off the gas valve!" Tanner yelled from a safe distance.

"We will do nothing of the sort!" the White Wizard bellowed.

"Look what you've done. You're going to set the whole forest ablaze!"

"Hmm, seems to me it was one of you meddling kids that

caused that little distraction. No matter, I just wish it was me that came up with that idea!"

Tanner ignored the older man's words. Like the fire surrounding them, the White Wizard's words licked about fiendishly. Harry Eaglesmith, standing beside him as the words spread around him like a flame, was transfixed.

What is wrong with him? Tanner thought. *Why can't he see through it?*

He closed his eyes, calmed his breathing and stretched his conscious mind out into the space that Harry occupied. As he did, he immediately saw the challenge: holding Harry's shoulders, whispering into his ear and assuming the human form of the White Wizard was Malsum, Glooscap's brother.

Malsum needed the beacon Harry provided to manifest himself in the physical world. Harry was the unwitting medium who'd been corrupted to serve the spiritual world. To save the river, Tanner would need to break the bond.

"Brother Glooscap!" Malsum bellowed.

Tanner stayed within himself and did not answer.

"Clever, young child. Clever. You know you are not a god and so don't pretend to be," Malsum continued.

Tanner could think of no retort. But maybe that was Malsum's ploy. Tanner turned away. His mind reached instead to the spirit of every living thing he could imagine. Malsum, sensing the plan, started to grow. He rose up, his form growing larger, ready to charge the young upstart.

The ground under both combatants thundered in anticipation. Tanner was about to meet his nemesis when the first speck of rain kissed his cheek, a reminder from the material world that other forces were working to save the forest. Tanner flinched and back-pedalled, a thought taking form.

I've got to keep him occupied!

As Tanner looked around for a source for his influence he was blindsided by a murder of crows. They swept in from behind and thundered him to the ground.

The White Wizard cackled, his form growing still larger.

Tanner gained his senses before he got an idea. Those infinitesimally small creatures rose from the forest floor. An old rotting tree, littered with ants, insects and other creatures, broke from the earth and clubbed the White Wizard to the ground.

Tanner turned to witness the great eagle, the lord of the sky, circling in greater speed. The crows, still attempting to menace Tanner, squawked and scattered. The rain, growing more intense and forceful, was slowing the fire, but not enough to snuff it completely.

The crows, swooping away from the young boy on the forest floor, gathered instead to attack the circle of birds in the sky. The formation broke. The winds subsided. Tanner gazed at the White Wizard who struggled to regain his feet. The fire, once slowing, approached its previous velocity.

Was there nothing more he could do? He had command of the air and the earth and still it wasn't enough. What more could he do? He looked around desperately.

The heat of the river scattered fish who leapt out of the water in despair.

"That's it!" Tanner exclaimed. He turned away from the forest and the sky. He reached out to the river.

Seals, crab, lobster, salmon, eels, crawfish, sharks, all the creatures that moved in the sea, gathered at the mouth of the river of fire. Feeling the pain of the suffering it was made to endure, the animals swam up river. As more aquatic creatures joined the colony, the first ripple of water started to break the surface.

Locals who would later describe the event noted the water seemed to grow into a rogue wave right in the heart of the river. And indeed, it did. From tributaries, streams and ponds, the momentum built and grew along the deep channel of the river of fire. But the most important thing was the crest. If the momentum peaked too early or too late, the fire would merely ride the wave until the energy diminished. The wave would need to peak at just the right moment to starve the fire of oxygen and put out the blaze.

"Crank it up boys. Use the throttle. Keep it wide open." But as Roy spit the words over the radio, he knew it was pointless. There was no way they could hear his voice over the roar of the engine. Instead, from under the tower, Roy waved his hands, urging more wind.

Riley, Donovan and Marshal held onto the machines with all their might. The large motor spun the massive fan and launched the rain toward the fire in the middle of the river. The fire was slowly starting to lose its mettle. But there was a dogged persistence that prevented it from being completely quashed. Roy looked at his towers, spewing rain in a concentrated cone. The fans lifted the rain far out into the river, pelting the flames back to the source. His plan was working, but until the source of fuel was turned off, he could only hope to contain the fire.

It was the rain that managed to get through to Tanner and

give him his fateful idea. With two adults standing guard by the valve at the reservoir it was a pointless fight, especially as one grew larger by the minute. Even with all of Glooscap's resources at his disposal, it was a stalemate. Those small woodland creatures, valiant in their defense of their habitat, could only hope to keep the White Wizard engaged for so long.

So far as Tanner could tell, whatever spiritual connection had been awakened, stretched much farther than he could imagine. Those forces were now acting unto themselves.

Except the heavy rain that was now starting to drench the forest. It had become an unwelcome distraction to the White Wizard. A foreign element to the feud.

But also an element of realism that Tanner forgot. Trusting the actions he set in motion would continue without his influence, Tanner stepped out of that realm of consciousness. The White Wizard, fixated on destruction, failed to notice his quarry no longer shared his realm.

With simple aplomb, Tanner marched next to Harry Eagle-smith and set a hand on his shoulder.

"We've awakened the River of Fire, Harry," Tanner whispered into his ear. At the moment Tanner's hand touched Harry's shoulder, Harry shuddered. His body startled.

"I hear sirens," Harry said in halted speech.

"They'll think we're terrorists," Tanner pleaded.

"Because you are!" the White Wizard bellowed. He charged down from where he was standing.

Breaking formation, the great eagle swooped down, talons extended. A piercing shriek confounded the White Wizard. The spiritual bond had been broken, the protective veil lifted. No longer were the animals of the forest divided. Raven. Crow. Blackbird. All took their moment to attack the White Wizard and chase him from the forest.

Tanner, seizing Harry's hand, pulled him to the valve. They managed to reach it just as the aquatic creatures halted their forward momentum. A crashing surf, once heard only along the shores of the great ocean, could be heard all along the river of fire. The wave peaked and crashed at just the right moment, rolling water all about the diminished fire. It was as if a hand reached up from the bottom of the river and pulled the flame back down to the depths from which it originated. The last flicker of unholy fire dissipated under a swirling torrent of current. The face of Malsum died out in the depths below.

15

The Suspicious Officer

The forest continued to swarm with firemen and emergency personnel. They dispatched themselves to put out some of the smaller, more troublesome flames that continued to persist. A dense smoke still hung in the air. The heat of the fire slowly released its grip on the woods.

"I managed to get my smart phone working and contacted 911," Donovan said with confidence. He was engaged with a police detective and several uniformed officers. The detective, old and grizzled, was skeptical. His jaw clenched as he heard the story.

The young officers were enraptured.

"Hey, wait a minute," Marshal said as he overheard the conversation, "is my son a suspect?"

"No chance, sir. With the quick thinking of these brave young men, we've been able to locate this illegal operation and report it to the proper authorities," the policeman said. "The entire confession has been recorded by our service and will be rendered as admissible evidence."

The detective folded up his notepad and stomped away in a huff. He shook his head as he stormed off. The rest of the officers shrugged. From his police car, the detective threw his notepad against the dash.

"I guess not everyone feels the same way," Roy commented.

Marshal turned to his son, a broad grin spread across his face.

"You should be proud of what they did. They're heroes!" the police officer continued. "And hey, we might just issue a citation and make all three of them honorary deputies."

"You can do that?" Tanner asked. Riley's ears perked up.

"All three?" Tanner continued, noticing Kim being tended to at the back of an ambulance. "but there's four of us."

Out of the corner of his eye, Tanner noticed the police detective in the car burning his eyes at him. Tanner wanted to lock eyes immediately, but thought better than to advertise his new talents. He grinned at the older man before noticing the name badge.

"That's just old man Thompson," Riley said. "He's always got a beef with somebody. He's just jealous we've done more in two days than he has in his entire career."

"Don't worry, Riley, I've got an eye on him," Tanner said.

The boys blushed, their fathers beamed with pride.

"This is incredible. You mean to tell me I still have to go work for that old fossil!?" Tanner said, exasperated.

Warren sighed. He knew this wouldn't be an easy subject to broach. The boys had been the toast of the town for a week. Media coverage had spread beyond the confines of Whispering Cove. Local and national crews shared tales of their exploits and the adoration was a little...much. Though they'd acquitted themselves well during the adventure, the volume of attention had, not surprisingly, swelled their egos a little bit. Warren got a little of the same treatment, being the father responsible for such heroic virtues. He could easily see how it might sink a little deep. Frankly, it would be good for his son to be humbled again.

"Tanner, this is another matter. You caused the damage. Just as the men you exposed will be punished, and hopefully LEARN from that, so too must you. Being a hero isn't always about cameras and adoration. It's about doing the right thing when you know it's the right thing to do, even if it's not what you want to do," Warren explained.

Tanner was hardly convinced. The rest of the trip was spent in silence. Warren hoped his counseling had some positive effect. The grunt Tanner made when he left the car suggested otherwise.

The late summer sun was restless. It seemed to linger forever in the horizon. Tanner looked up at it the tenth time in the past five minutes and cursed his fate. He flopped the wheelbarrow down heavily to the ground. A clay pot rolled from the top of the pile of pulled weeds, hit the interlocking driveway and cracked neatly in half.

"Aww blett!" Tanner spewed in French.

"You get that language from your father?" the old lady asked.

"Uh, Mrs. Inglett, you surprised me. I thought you were in the house?" Tanner stammered.

"Well, I wasn't. Should I add that broken pot onto your tab? If you keep this up, I'll have my entire garden weeded. My gardener will be very impressed. He might even hire you to work in his place," Mrs. Inglett said.

"You already have a gardener?" Tanner muttered.

"And a butler, a chef and chauffeur."

"What, no maid?"

"I haven't sought fit to replace her yet. The role is available, if you think you might be interested," Hazel Inglett offered.

"If you have all these people do everything for you, what do you do all day?"

"You mean you don't know? I thought it was the worst kept secret in town."

"I'm twelve, why would I?"

Mrs. Inglett gazed at him intently for a moment before answering.

"I heard a little bit about your exploits at the river the other day. Hard not to, really. Did you do all of those things, or did your father somehow make a hero out of you?"

It was a deliberate jab. Tanner seethed. He wanted to yell and scream. Throw a tantrum at the injustice of this situation. Instead he collected himself. He gathered his breath. He looked away momentarily before locking eyes with the old lady.

The grey mist was starting to descend around them when Mrs. Inglett closed her eyes and shook her head. In an instant, the shroud lost its grip and quickly disappeared.

"What!?!" Mrs. Inglett stammered before her legs wobbled. Tanner jumped and caught her as she collapsed to the ground.

"My child," she stammered, "what on earth?"

"I don't know. It happened when we were out in the forest."

"That's some gift. Though something tells me you shouldn't advertise it. That settles it," she said.

"Settles what?"

Mrs. Inglett took a moment before speaking.

"If you want, you can keep coming here. Keep doing your little bit around the yard. Gill would be very happy with that.

Or..." she said and paused.

"Or?" Tanner fancied the possibilities that didn't include manual labour.

"Or we could find out where those talents could take us," Mrs. Inglett said.

"But I'm not a superhero," Tanner confessed.

"My boy, your father sought to challenge you to be the best you can be. And you did. And you succeeded. Wouldn't it be a shame to want to know more but be too afraid to find out?"

Tanner considered her words carefully.

"In my spare time, of which I have plenty, I do a little research. I have plenty of resources at my disposal. Unfortunately, my work is incomplete. I've grown old and unable to follow the leads I've found. I've uncovered some fascinating things. Some of those things make for great stories. And some of those stories still have many unanswered questions...."

The End

Jason E. Hamilton was a film lighting technician in 2001 when he met his wife, Sylvie Mazerolle, while working on a film in Saint John, New Brunswick. Later that year she moved to Toronto where they began their cemented their relationship.

Two days before Christmas in 2007 the couple received some startling news: Sylvie was pregnant with their first (and only) child.

In 2010 the young family sold their house in Toronto and made the permanent move to New Brunswick. The challenge was chronicled in Mr. Hamilton's debut book "Life, the Yurt and Everything" which he published in 2013.

Jason lives in Dieppe, New Brunswick with Sylvie and their son Dustin.

Tanner and the boys will return in "The Prince of Acadia & the Lost Tribe". To be released: spring 2017.

For more information please visit:

WWW.JASONEHAMILTON.CO